FRECKLES

FRECKLES

BY

GENE STRATTON-PORTER

AUTHOR OF

HER FATHER'S DAUGHTER,
A DAUGHTER OF THE LAND
THE WHITE FLAG, ETC.

GROSSET & DUNLAP
PUBLISHERS NEW YORK

Made in the United States of America

CL

PRINTED IN THE UNITED STATES
AT
THE COUNTRY LIFE PRESS, GARDEN CITY, N. Y.

TO

ALL GOOD IRISHMEN
IN GENERAL
AND ONE
CHARLES DARWIN PORTER
IN PARTICULAR

CONTENTS

CHARACTERS

FRECKLES, a Plucky Waif Who Guards the Limberlost Timber Leases and Dreams of Angels.

THE SWAMP ANGEL, in Whom Freckles' Sweetest Dream Materializes.

MCLEAN, a Member of a Grand Rapids Lumber Company, Who Befriends Freckles.

MRS. DUNCAN, Who Gives Mother-love and a Home to Freckles.

DUNCAN, Head Teamster of McLean's Timber Gang.

LORD and LADY O'MORE, Who Come from Ireland in Quest of a Lost Relative.

THE MAN OF AFFAIRS, Brusque of Manner, but Big of Heart.

WESSNER, a Dutch Timber-thief Who Wants Rascality Made Easy.

BLACK JACK, a Villain to Whom Thought of Repentance Comes too Late.

SEARS, Camp Cook.

CHAPTER I

Wherein Great Risks Are Taken and the Limberlost Guard Is Hired

FRECKLES

CHAPTER I

Wherein Great Risks Are Taken and the Limberlost Guard Is Hired

FRECKLES came down the corduroy that crosses the lower end of the Limberlost. At a glance he might have been mistaken for a tramp, but he was truly seeking work. He was intensely eager to belong somewhere and to be attached to almost any enterprise that would furnish him food and clothing.

Long before he came in sight of the camp of the Grand Rapids Lumber Company, he could hear the cheery voices of the men, the neighing of the horses, and could scent the tempting odours of cooking food. A feeling of homeless friendlessness swept over him in a sickening wave. Without stopping to think, he turned into the newly made road and followed it to the camp, where the gang was making ready for supper and bed.

The scene was intensely attractive. The thickness of the swamp made a dark, massive background below, while above towered gigantic trees. The men were calling jovially back and forth as they unharnessed tired horses that fell into attitudes of rest and crunched, in deep content, the grain given them. Duncan, the brawny

Scotch head-teamster, lovingly wiped the flanks of his big bays with handfuls of pawpaw leaves, as he softly whistled, "O wha will be my dearie, O!" and a cricket beneath the leaves at his feet accompanied him. The green wood fire hissed and crackled merrily. Wreathing tongues of flame wrapped around the big black kettles, and when the cook lifted the lids to plunge in his testing-fork, gusts of savoury odours escaped.

Freckles approached him.

"I want to speak with the Boss," he said.

The cook glanced at him and answered carelessly: "He can't use you."

The colour flooded Freckles' face, but he said simply: "If you will be having the goodness to point him out, we will give him a chance to do his own talking."

With a shrug of astonishment, the cook led the way to a rough board table where a broad, square-shouldered man was bending over some account-books.

"Mr. McLean, here's another man wanting to be taken on the gang, I suppose," he said.

"All right," came the cheery answer. "I never needed a good man more than I do just now."

The manager turned a page and carefully began a new line.

"No use of your bothering with this fellow," volunteered the cook. "He hasn't but one hand."

The flush on Freckles' face burned deeper. His lips thinned to a mere line. He lifted his shoulders, took a step forward, and thrust out his right arm, from which the sleeve dangled empty at the wrist.

"That will do, Sears," came the voice of the Boss sharply. "I will interview my man when I finish this report."

He turned to his work, while the cook hurried to the fires. Freckles stood one instant as he had braced himself to meet the eyes of the manager; then his arm dropped and a wave of whiteness swept him. The Boss had not even turned his head. He had used the possessive. When he said "my man," the hungry heart of Freckles went reaching toward him.

The boy drew a quivering breath. Then he whipped off his old hat and beat the dust from it carefully. With his left hand he caught the right sleeve, wiped his sweaty face, and tried to straighten his hair with his fingers. He broke a spray of ironwort beside him and used the purple bloom to beat the dust from his shoulders and limbs. The Boss, busy over his report, was, nevertheless, vaguely alive to the toilet being made behind him, and scored one for the man.

McLean was a Scotchman. It was his habit to work slowly and methodically. The men of his camps never had known him to be in a hurry or to lose his temper. Discipline was inflexible, but the Boss was always kind. His habits were simple. He shared camp life with his gangs. The only visible signs of wealth consisted of a big, shimmering diamond stone of ice and fire that glittered and burned on one of his fingers, and the dainty, beautiful thoroughbred mare he rode between camps and across the country on business.

No man of McLean's gangs could honestly say that he

ever had been overdriven or underpaid. The Boss never had exacted any deference from his men, yet so intense was his personality that no man of them ever had attempted a familiarity. They all knew him to be a thorough gentleman, and that in the great timber city several millions stood to his credit.

He was the only son of that McLean who had sent out the finest ships ever built in Scotland. That his son should carry on this business after the father's death had been his ambition. He had sent the boy through the universities of Oxford and Edinburgh, and allowed him several years' travel before he should attempt his first commission for the firm.

Then he was ordered to southern Canada and Michigan to purchase a consignment of tall, straight timber for masts, and south to Indiana for oak beams. The young man entered these mighty forests, parts of which lay untouched since the dawn of the morning of time. The clear, cool, pungent atmosphere was intoxicating. The intense silence, like that of a great empty cathedral, fascinated him. He gradually learned that, to the shy wood creatures that darted across his path or peeped inquiringly from leafy ambush, he was brother. He found himself approaching, with a feeling of reverence, those majestic trees that had stood through ages of sun, wind, and snow. Soon it became difficult to fell them. When he had filled his order and returned home, he was amazed to learn that in the swamps and forests he had lost his heart and it was calling—forever calling him.

When he inherited his father's property, he promptly

disposed of it, and, with his mother, founded a home in a splendid residence in the outskirts of Grand Rapids. With three partners, he organized a lumber company. His work was to purchase, fell, and ship the timber to the mills. Marshall managed the milling process and passed the lumber to the factory. From the lumber, Barthol made beautiful and useful furniture, which Uptegrove scattered all over the world from a big wholesale house. Of the thousands who saw their faces reflected on the polished surfaces of that furniture and found comfort in its use, few there were to whom it suggested mighty forests and trackless swamps, and the man, big of soul and body, who cut his way through them, and with the eye of experience doomed the proud trees that were now entering the homes of civilization for service.

When McLean turned from his finished report, he faced a young man, yet under twenty, tall, spare, heavily framed, closely freckled, and red-haired, with a homely Irish face, but in the steady gray eyes, straightly meeting his searching ones of blue, there was unswerving candour and the appearance of longing not to be ignored. He was dressed in the roughest of farm clothing, and seemed tired to the point of falling.

"You are looking for work?" questioned McLean.

"Yis," answered Freckles.

"I am very sorry," said the Boss with genuine sympathy in his every tone, "but there is only one man I want at present—a hardy, big fellow with a stout heart and a strong body. I hoped that you would do, but I am afraid you are too young and scarcely strong enough."

Freckles stood, hat in hand, watching McLean.

"And what was it you thought I might be doing?" he asked.

The Boss could scarcely repress a start. Somewhere before accident and poverty there had been an ancestor who used cultivated English, even with an accent. The boy spoke in a mellow Irish voice, sweet and pure. It was scarcely definite enough to be called brogue, yet there was a trick in the turning of the sentence, the wrong sound of a letter here and there, that was almost irresistible to McLean, and presaged a misuse of infinitives and possessives with which he was very familiar and which touched him nearly. He was of foreign birth, and despite years of alienation, in times of strong feeling he committed inherited sins of accent and construction.

"It's no child's job," answered McLean. "I am the field manager of a big lumber company. We have just leased two thousand acres of the Limberlost. Many of these trees are of great value. We can't leave our camp, six miles south, for almost a year yet; so we have blazed a trail and strung barbed wires securely around this lease. Before we return to our work, I must put this property in the hands of a reliable, brave, strong man who will guard it every hour of the day, and sleep with one eye open at night. I shall require the entire length of the trail to be walked at least twice each day, to make sure that our lines are up and that no one has been trespassing."

Freckles was leaning forward, absorbing every word with such intense eagerness that he was beguiling the Boss into explanations he had never intended making.

"But why wouldn't that be the finest job in the world for me?" he pleaded. "I am never sick. I could walk the trail twice, three times every day, and I'd be watching sharp all the while."

"It's because you are scarcely more than a boy, and this will be a trying job for a work-hardened man," answered McLean. "You see, in the first place, you would be afraid. In stretching our lines, we killed six rattlesnakes almost as long as your body and as thick as your arm. It's the price of your life to start through the marsh-grass surrounding the swamp unless you are covered with heavy leather above your knees.

"You should be able to swim in case high water undermines the temporary bridge we have built where Sleepy Snake Creek enters the swamp. The fall and winter changes of weather are abrupt and severe, while I would want strict watch kept every day. You would always be alone, and I don't guarantee what is in the Limberlost. It is lying here as it has laid since the beginning of time, and it is alive with forms and voices. I don't pretend to say what all of them come from; but from a few slinking shapes I've seen, and hair-raising yells I've heard, I'd rather not confront their owners myself; and I am neither weak nor fearful.

"Worst of all, any man who will enter the swamp to mark and steal timber is desperate. One of my employees at the south camp, John Carter, compelled me to discharge him for a number of serious reasons. He came here, entered the swamp alone, and succeeded in locating and marking a number of valuable trees that he was endeavouring to sell to a rival company when we secured the lease. He has sworn to have these trees if he has to die or to kill others to get them; and he is a man that the strongest would not care to meet."

"But if he came to steal trees, wouldn't he bring teams and men enough: that all any one could do would be to watch and be after you?" queried the boy.

"Yes," replied McLean.

"Then why couldn't I be watching just as closely, and coming as fast, as an older, stronger man?" asked Freckles.

"Why, by George, you could!" exclaimed McLean. "I don't know as the size of a man would be half so important as his grit and faithfulness, come to think of it. Sit on that log there and we will talk it over. What is your name?"

Freckles shook his head at the proffer of a seat, and folding his arms, stood straight as the trees around him. He grew a shade whiter, but his eyes never faltered.

"Freckles!" he said.

"Good enough for everyday," laughed McLean, "but I scarcely can put 'Freckles' on the company's books. Tell me your name."

"I haven't any name," replied the boy.

"I don't understand," said McLean.

"I was thinking from the voice and the face of you that you wouldn't," said Freckles, slowly. "I've spent more time on it than I ever did on anything else in all me life, and I don't understand. Does it seem to you that any one would take a new-born baby and row over it, until it was bruised black, cut off its hand, and leave it out in a bitter night on the steps of a charity home, to the care of strangers? That's what somebody did to me."

McLean stared aghast. He had no reply ready, and presently in a low voice he suggested: "And after——?"

"The Home people took me in, and I was there the full legal age and several years over. For the most part we were a lot of little Irishmen together. They could always find homes for the other children, but nobody would ever be wanting me on account of me arm."

"Were they kind to you?" McLean regretted the question the minute it was asked.

"I don't know," answered Freckles. The reply sounded so hopeless, even to his own ears, that he hastened to qualify it by adding: "You see, it's like this, sir. Kindnesses that people are paid to lay off in job lots and that belong equally to several hundred others, ain't going to be soaking into any one fellow so much."

"Go on," said McLean, nodding comprehendingly.

"There's nothing worth the taking of your time to tell," replied Freckles. "The Home was in Chicago, and I was there all me life until three months ago. When I was too old for the training they gave to the little children, they sent me to the closest ward school as long as the law would let them; but I was never like any of the other children, and they all knew it. I'd to go and come like a prisoner, and be working around the Home early and late for me board and clothes. I always wanted to learn mighty bad, but I was glad when that was over.

"Every few days, all me life, I'd to be called up, looked over, and refused a home and love, on account of me hand

and ugly face; but it was all the home I'd ever known, and I didn't seem to belong to any place else.

"Then a new superintendent was put in. He wasn't for being like any of the others, and he swore he'd weed me out the first thing he did. He made a plan to send me down the State to a man he said he knew who needed a boy. He wasn't for remembering to tell that man that I was a hand short, and he knocked me down the minute he found I was the boy who had been sent him. Between noon and that evening, he and his son close my age had me in pretty much the same shape in which I was found in the beginning, so I lay awake that night and ran away. I'd like to have squared me account with that boy before I left, but I didn't dare for fear of waking the old man, and I knew I couldn't handle the two of them; but I'm hoping to meet him alone some day before I die."

McLean tugged at his moustache to hide the smile on his lips, but he liked the boy all the better for this confession.

"I didn't even have to steal clothes to get rid of starting in me Home ones," Freckles continued, "for they had already taken all me clean, neat things for the boy and put me into his rags, and that went almost as sore as the beatings, for where I was we were always kept tidy and sweet-smelling, anyway. I hustled clear into this State before I learned that man couldn't have kept me if he'd wanted to. When I thought I was good and away from him, I commenced hunting work, but it is with everybody else just as it is with you, sir. Big, strong, whole men are the only ones for being wanted."

"I have been studying over this matter," answered

McLean. "I am not so sure but that a man no older than you and similar in every way could do this work very well, if he were not a coward, and had it in him to be trustworthy and industrious."

Freckles came forward a step.

"If you will give me a job where I can earn me food, clothes, and a place to sleep," he said, "if I can have a Boss to work for like other men, and a place I feel I've a right to, I will do precisely what you tell me or die trying."

He spoke so convincingly that McLean believed, although in his heart he knew that to employ a stranger would be wretched business for a man with the interests he had involved.

"Very well," the Boss found himself answering, "I will enter you on my pay-rolls. We'll have supper, and then I will provide you with clean clothing, wading-boots, the wire-mending apparatus, and a revolver. The first thing in the morning, I will take you the length of the trail myself and explain fully what I want done. All I ask of you is to come to me at once at the south camp and tell me as a man if you find this job too hard for you. It will not surprise me. It is work that few men would perform faithfully. What name shall I put down?"

Freckles' gaze never left McLean's face, and the Boss saw the swift spasm of pain that swept his lonely, sensitive features.

"I haven't any name," he said stubbornly, "no more than one somebody clapped on to me when they put me on the Home books, with not the thought or care they'd name a house cat. I've seen how they enter those poor, little abandoned devils often enough to know. What they called me is no more my name than it is yours. I don't know what mine is, and I never will; but I am going to be your man and do your work, and I'll be glad to answer to any name you choose to call me. Won't you please be giving me a name, Mr. McLean?"

The Boss wheeled abruptly and began stacking his books. What he was thinking was probably what any other gentleman would have thought in the circumstances. With his eyes still downcast, and in a voice harsh with huskiness, he spoke.

"I will tell you what we will do, my lad," he said. "My father was my ideal man, and I loved him better than any other I have ever known. He went out five years ago, but that he would have been proud to leave you his name I firmly believe. If I give to you the name of my nearest kin and the man I loved best—will that do?"

Freckles' rigid attitude relaxed suddenly. His head dropped, and big tears splashed on the soiled calico shirt. McLean was not surprised at the silence, for he found that talking came none too easily just then.

"All right," he said. "I will write it on the roll—James Ross McLean."

"Thank you mightily," said Freckles. "That makes me feel almost as if I belonged, already."

"You do," said McLean. "Until some one armed with every right comes to claim you, you are mine. Now, come and take a bath, have some supper, and go to bed."

As Freckles followed into the lights and sounds of the camp, his heart and soul were singing for joy.

CHAPTER II

Wherein Freckles Proves His Mettle and Finds Friends

CHAPTER II

Wherein Freckles Proves His Mettle and Finds Friends

NEXT morning found Freckles in clean, whole clothing, fed, and rested. Then McLean outfitted him and gave him careful instruction in the use of his weapon. The Boss showed him around the timber-line, and engaged him a place to board with the family of his head-teamster, Duncan, whom he had brought from Scotland with him, and who lived in a small clearing he was working out between the swamp and the corduroy. When the gang was started for the south camp, Freckles was left to guard a fortune in the Limberlost. That he was under guard himself those first weeks he never knew.

Each hour was torture to the boy. The restricted life of a great city orphanage was the other extreme of the world compared with the Limberlost. He was afraid for his life every minute. The heat was intense. The heavy wading-boots rubbed his feet until they bled. He was sore and stiff from his long tramp and outdoor exposure. The seven miles of trail was agony at every step. He practised at night, under the direction of Duncan, until he grew sure in the use of his revolver. He cut a stout hickory cudgel, with a knot on the end as big as his fist;

this never left his hand. What he thought in those first days he himself could not recall clearly afterward.

His heart stood still every time he saw the beautiful marsh-grass begin a sinuous waving *against* the play of the wind, as McLean had told him it would. He bolted half a mile with the first boom of the bittern, and his hat lifted with every yelp of the sheitpoke. Once he saw a lean, shadowy form following him, and fired his revolver. Then he was frightened worse than ever for fear it might have been Duncan's collie.

The first afternoon that he found his wires down, and he was compelled to plunge knee deep into the black swamp-muck to restring them, he became so ill from fear and nervousness that he scarcely could control his shaking hand to do the work. With every step, he felt that he would miss secure footing and be swallowed in that clinging sea of blackness. In dumb agony he plunged forward, clinging to the posts and trees until he had finished restringing and testing the wire. He had consumed much time. Night closed in. The Limberlost stirred gently, then shook herself, growled, and awoke around him.

There seemed to be a great owl hooting from every hollow tree, and a little one screeching from every knot-hole. The bellowing of big bullfrogs was not sufficiently deafening to shut out the wailing of whip-poor-wills that seemed to come from every bush. Night-hawks swept past him with their shivering cry, and bats struck his face. A prowling wild cat missed its catch and screamed with rage. A straying fox bayed incessantly for its mate.

The hair on the back of Freckles' neck arose as bristles,

and his knees wavered beneath him. He could not see whether the dreaded snakes were on the trail, or, in the pandemonium, hear the rattle for which McLean had cautioned him to listen. He stood motionless in an agony of fear. His breath whistled between his teeth. The perspiration ran down his face and body in little streams.

Something big, black, and heavy came crashing through the swamp close to him, and with a yell of utter panic Freckles ran—how far he did not know; but at last he gained control over himself and retraced his steps. His jaws set stiffly and the sweat dried on his body. When he reached the place from which he had started to run, he turned and with measured steps made his way down the line. After a time he realized that he was only walking, so he faced that sea of horrors again. When he came toward the corduroy, the cudgel fell to test the wire at each step.

Sounds that curdled his blood seemed to encompass him, and shapes of terror to draw closer and closer. Fear had so gained the mastery that he did not dare look behind him; and just when he felt that he would fall dead before he ever reached the clearing, came Duncan's rolling call: "Freckles! Freckles!" A shuddering sob burst in the boy's dry throat; but he only told Duncan that finding the wire down had caused the delay.

The next morning he started on time. Day after day, with his heart pounding, he ducked, dodged, ran when he could, and fought when he was brought to bay. If he ever had an idea of giving up, no one knew it; for he clung to his job without the shadow of wavering. All these things, in so far as he guessed them, Duncan, who had been set to watch the first weeks of Freckles' work, carried to the Boss at the south camp; but the innermost, exquisite torture of the thing the big Scotchman never guessed, and McLean, with his finer perceptions, came only a little closer.

After a few weeks, when Freckles learned that he was still living, that he had a home, and the very first money he ever had possessed was safe in his pockets, he began to grow proud. He yet side stepped, dodged, and hurried to avoid being late again, but he was gradually developing the fearlessness that men ever acquire of dangers to which they are hourly accustomed.

His heart seemed to be leaping when his first rattler disputed the trail with him, but he mustered courage to attack it with his club. After its head had been crushed, he mastered an Irishman's inborn repugnance for snakes sufficiently to cut off its rattles to show Duncan. With this victory, his greatest fear of them was gone.

Then he began to realize that with the abundance of food in the swamp, flesh-hunters would not come on the trail and attack him, and he had his revolver for defence if they did. He soon learned to laugh at the big, floppy birds that made horrible noises. One day, watching behind a tree, he saw a crane solemnly performing a few measures of a belated nuptial song-and-dance with his mate. Realizing that it was intended in tenderness, no matter how it appeared, the lonely, starved heart of the boy sympathized with them.

Before the first month passed, he was fairly easy about his job; by the next he rather liked it. Nature can be trusted to work her own miracle in the heart of any man whose daily task keeps him alone among her sights, sounds, and silences.

When day after day the only thing that relieved his utter loneliness was the companionship of the birds and beasts of the swamp, it was the most natural thing in the world that Freckles should turn to them for friendship. He began by instinctively protecting the weak and helpless. He was astonished at the quickness with which they became accustomed to him and the disregard they showed for his movements, when they learned that he was not a hunter, while the club he carried was used more frequently for their benefit than his own. He scarcely could believe what he saw.

From the effort to protect the birds and animals, it was only a short step to the possessive feeling, and with that sprang the impulse to caress and provide. Through fall, when brooding was finished and the upland birds sought the swamp in swarms to feast on its seeds and berries, Freckles was content with watching them and speculating about them. Outside of half a dozen of the very commonest they were strangers to him. The likeness of their actions to humanity was an hourly surprise.

When black frost began stripping the Limberlost, cutting the ferns, shearing the vines from the trees, mowing the succulent green things of the swale, and setting the leaves swirling down, he watched the departing troops of his friends with dismay. He began to realize that he would be left alone. He made especial efforts toward friendliness with the hope that he could induce some of them to stay. It was then that he conceived the idea of carrying food to the birds; for he saw that they were leaving for lack of it; but he could not stop them. Day after day, flocks gathered and departed: by the time the first snow whitened his trail around the Limberlost, there were left only the little black-and-white juncos, the sapsuckers, yellowhammers, a few patriarchs among the flaming cardinals, the blue jays, the crows, and the quail.

Then Freckles began his wizard work. He cleared a space of swale, and twice a day he spread a birds' banquet. By the middle of December the strong winds of winter had beaten most of the seed from the grass and bushes. The snow fell, covering the swamp, and food was very scarce and difficult to find. The birds scarcely waited until Freckles' back was turned to attack his provisions. In a few weeks they flew toward the clearing to meet him. During the bitter weather of January they came half-way to the cabin every morning, and fluttered around him as doves all the way to the feeding-ground. Before February they were so accustomed to him, and so hunger-driven, that they would perch on his head and shoulders, and the saucy jays would try to pry into his pockets.

Then Freckles added to wheat and crumbs, every scrap of refuse food he could find at the cabin. He carried to his pets the parings of apples, turnips, potatoes, stray cabbage-leaves, and carrots, and tied to the bushes meat-bones having scraps of fat and gristle. One morning, coming to his feeding-ground unusually early, he found a gorgeous cardinal and a rabbit side by side sociably nibbling a cabbage-leaf, and that instantly gave to him the idea of cracking nuts, from the store he had gathered for Duncan's children, for the squirrels, in the effort to add them to his family. Soon he had them coming—red, gray, and black; then he became filled with a vast impatience that he did not know their names or habits.

So the winter passed. Every week McLean rode to the Limberlost; never on the same day or at the same hour. Always he found Freckles at his work, faithful and brave, no matter how severe the weather.

The boy's earnings constituted his first money; and when the Boss explained to him that he could leave them safe at a bank and carry away a scrap of paper that represented the amount, he went straight on every pay-day and made his deposit, keeping out barely what was necessary for his board and clothing. What he wanted to do with his money he did not know, but it gave to him a sense of freedom and power to feel that it was there—it was his and he could have it when he chose. In imitation of McLean, he bought a small pocket account-book, in which he carefully set down every dollar he earned and every penny he spent. As his expenses were small and the Boss paid him generously, it was astonishing how his little hoard grew.

That winter held the first hours of real happiness in Freckles' life. He was free. He was doing a man's work faithfully, through every rigour of rain, snow, and blizzard. He was gathering a wonderful strength of body, paying his way, and saving money. Every man of the gang and of that locality knew that he was under the protection of McLean, who was a power; this had the effect of smoothing Freckles' path in many directions.

Mrs. Duncan showed him that individual kindness for

which his hungry heart was longing. She had a hot drink ready for him when he came from a freezing day on the trail. She knit him a heavy mitten for his left hand, and devised a way to sew and pad the right sleeve that protected the maimed arm in bitter weather. She patched his clothing—frequently torn by the wire—and saved kitchen-scraps for his birds, not because she either knew or cared anything about them, but because she herself was close enough to the swamp to be touched by its utter loneliness. When Duncan laughed at her for this, she retorted: "My God, mannie, if Freckles hadna the birds and the beasts he would be always alone. It was never meant for a human being to be so solitary. He'd get touched in the head if he hadna them to think for and to talk to."

"How much answer do ye think he gets to his talkin', lass?" laughed Duncan.

"He gets the answer that keeps the eye bricht, the heart happy, and the feet walking faithful the rough path he's set them in," answered Mrs. Duncan earnestly.

Duncan walked away appearing very thoughtful. The next morning he gave an ear from the corn he was shelling for his chickens to Freckles, and told him to carry it to his wild chickens in the Limberlost. Freckles laughed delightedly.

"Me chickens!" he said. "Why didn't I ever think of that before? Of course they are! They are just little, brightly coloured cocks and hens! But 'wild' is no good. What would you say to me 'wild chickens' being a good deal tamer than yours here in your yard?"

"Hoot, lad!" cried Duncan.

"Make yours light on your head and eat out of your hands and pockets," challenged Freckles.

"Go and tell your fairy tales to the wee people! They're juist brash on believin' things," said Duncan. "Ye canna invent any story too big to stop them from callin' for a bigger."

"I dare you to come see!" retorted Freckles.

"Take ye!" said Duncan. "If ye make juist ane bird licht on your heid or eat frae your hand, ye are free to help yoursel' to my corn-crib and wheat-bin the rest of the winter."

Freckles sprang in air and howled in glee.

"Oh, Duncan! You're too aisy," he cried. "When will you come?"

"I'll come next Sabbath," said Duncan. "And I'll believe the birds of the Limberlost are tame as barnyard-fowl when I see it, and no sooner!"

After that Freckles always spoke of the birds as his chickens, and the Duncans followed his example. The very next Sabbath, Duncan, with his wife and children, followed Freckles to the swamp. They saw a sight so wonderful it will keep them talking all the remainder of their lives, and make them unfailing friends of all the birds.

Freckles' chickens were awaiting him at the edge of the clearing. They cut the frosty air around his head into curves and circles of crimson, blue, and black. They chased each other from Freckles, and swept so closely themselves that they brushed him with their outspread wings.

At their feeding-ground Freckles set down his old pail of scraps and swept the snow from a small level space with a broom improvised of twigs. As soon as his back was turned, the birds clustered over the food, snatching scraps to carry to the nearest bushes. Several of the boldest, a big crow and a couple of jays, settled on the rim and feasted at leisure, while a cardinal, that hesitated to venture, fumed and scolded from a twig overhead.

Then Freckles scattered his store. At once the ground resembled the spread mantle of Montezuma, except that this mass of gaily coloured feathers was on the backs of living birds. While they feasted, Duncan gripped his wife's arm and stared in astonishment; for from the bushes and dry grass, with gentle cheeping and queer, throaty chatter, as if to encourage each other, came flocks of quail. Before any one saw it arrive, a big gray rabbit sat in the midst of the feast, contentedly gnawing a cabbage-leaf.

"Weel, I be drawed on!" came Mrs. Duncan's tense whisper.

"Shu-shu," cautioned Duncan.

Lastly Freckles removed his cap. He began filling it with handfuls of wheat from his pockets. In a swarm the grain-eaters arose around him as a flock of tame pigeons. They perched on his arms and the cap, and in the stress of hunger, forgetting all caution, a brilliant cock cardinal and an equally gaudy jay fought for a perching-place on his head.

"Weel, I'm beat," muttered Duncan, forgetting the silence imposed on his wife. "I'll hae to give in. 'Seein' is believin'.' A man wad hae to see that to believe it

We mauna let the Boss miss that sight, for it's a chance will no likely come twice in a life. Everything is snowed under and thae craturs near starved, but trustin' Freckles that complete they are tamer than our chickens. Look hard, bairns!" he whispered. "Ye winna see the like o' yon again, while God lets ye live. Notice their colour against the ice and snow, and the pretty skippin' ways of them! And spunky! Weel, I'm beat fair!"

Freckles emptied his cap, turned his pockets and scattered his last grain. Then he waved his watching friends good-bye and started down the timber-line.

A week later, Duncan and Freckles arose from breakfast to face the bitterest morning of the winter. When Freckles, warmly capped and gloved, stepped to the corner of the kitchen for his scrap-pail, he found a big pan of steaming boiled wheat on the top of it. He wheeled to Mrs. Duncan with a shining face.

"Were you fixing this warm food for me chickens or yours?" he asked.

"It's for yours, Freckles," she said. "I was afeared this cold weather they wadna lay good without a warm bite now and then."

Duncan laughed as he stepped to the other room for his pipe; but Freckles faced Mrs. Duncan with a trace of every pang of starved mother-hunger he ever had suffered written large on his homely, splotched, narrow features.

"Oh, how I wish you were my mother!" he cried.

Mrs. Duncan attempted an echo of her husband's laugh.

"Lord love the lad!" she exclaimed. "Why, Freckles,

are ye no bricht enough to learn without being taught by a woman that I am your mither? If a great man like yoursel' dinna ken that, learn it now and ne'er forget it. Ance a woman is the wife of any man, she becomes wife to all men for having had the wifely experience she kens! Ance a man-child has beaten his way to life under the heart of a woman, she is mither to all men, for the hearts of mithers are everywhere the same. Bless ye, laddie, I am your mither!"

She tucked the coarse scarf she had knit for him closer over his chest and pulled his cap lower over his ears, but Freckles, whipping it off and holding it under his arm, caught her rough, reddened hand and pressed it to his lips in a long kiss. Then he hurried away to hide the happy, embarrassing tears that were coming straight from his swelling heart.

Mrs. Duncan, sobbing unrestrainedly, swept into the adjoining room and threw herself into Duncan's arms.

"Oh, the puir lad!" she wailed. "Oh, the puir mither-hungry lad! He breaks my heart!"

Duncan's arms closed convulsively around his wife. With a big, brown hand he lovingly stroked her rough, sorrel hair.

"Sarah, you're a guid woman!" he said. "You're a michty guid woman! Ye hae a way o' speakin' out at times that's like the inspired prophets of the Lord. If that had been put to me, now, I'd 'a' felt all I kent how to and been keen enough to say the richt thing; but dang it, I'd 'a' stuttered and stammered and got naething out that would ha' done onybody a mite o' good. But ye, Sarah!

Did ye see his face, woman? Ye sent him off lookin' leke a white light of holiness had passed ower and settled on him. Ye sent the lad away too happy for mortal words, Sarah. And ye made me that proud o' ye! I wouldna trade ye an' my share o' the Limberlost with ony king ye could mention."

He relaxed his clasp, and setting a heavy hand on each shoulder, he looked straight into her eyes.

"Ye're prime, Sarah! Juist prime!" he said.

Sarah Duncan stood alone in the middle of her two-roomed log-cabin and lifted a bony, claw-like pair of hands, reddened by frequent immersion in hot water, cracked and chafed by exposure to cold, black-lined by constant battle with swamp-loam, calloused with burns, and stared at them wonderingly.

"Pretty lookin' things ye are!" she whispered. "But ye hae juist been kissed. And by such a man! Fine as God ever made at His verra best. Duncan wouldna trade wi' a king! Na! Nor I wadna trade with a queen wi' a palace, an' velvet gowns, an' diamonds big as hazel-nuts, an' a hundred visitors a day into the bargain. Ye've been that honoured I'm blest if I can bear to souse ye in dish-water. Still, that kiss winna come off! Naething can take it from me, for it's mine till I dee. Lord, if I amna proud! Kisses on these old claws! Weel, I be drawed on!"

CHAPTER III

Wherein a Feather Falls and a Soul Is Born

CHAPTER III

WHEREIN A FEATHER FALLS AND A SOUL IS BORN

SO FRECKLES fared through the bitter winter. He was very happy. He had hungered for freedom, love, and appreciation so long! He had been unspeakably lonely at the Home; and the utter loneliness of a great desert or forest is not so difficult to endure as the loneliness of being constantly surrounded by crowds of people who do not care in the least whether one is living or dead.

All through the winter Freckles' entire energy was given to keeping up his lines and his "chickens" from freezing or starving. When the first breath of spring touched the Limberlost, and the snow receded before it; when the catkins began to bloom; when there came a hint of green to the trees, bushes, and swale; when the rushes lifted their heads, and the pulse of the newly resurrected season beat strongly in the heart of nature, something new stirred in the breast of the boy.

Nature always levies her tribute. Now she laid a powerful hand on the soul of Freckles, to which the boy's whole being responded, though he had not the least idea what was troubling him. Duncan accepted his wife's theory that it was a touch of spring fever, but Freckles knew better. He never had been so well. Clean, hot, and steady the blood pulsed in his veins. He was always hungry, and his most difficult work tired him not at all. For long months, without a single intermission, he had tramped those seven miles of trail twice each day, through every conceivable state of weather. With the heavy club he gave his wires a sure test, and between sections, first in play, afterward to keep his circulation going, he had acquired the skill of an expert drum-major. In his work there was exercise for every muscle of his body each hour of the day, at night a bath, wholesome food, and sound sleep in a room that never knew fire. He had gained flesh and colour, and developed a greater strength and endurance than any one ever could have guessed.

Nor did the Limberlost contain last year's terrors. He had been with her in her hour of desolation, when stripped bare and deserted, she had stood shivering, as if herself afraid. He had made excursions into the interior until he was familiar with every path and road that ever had been cut. He had sounded the depths of her deepest pools, and had learned why the trees grew so magnificently. He had found that places of swamp and swale were few compared with miles of solid timber-land, concealed by summer's luxuriant undergrowth.

The sounds that at first had struck cold fear into his soul he now knew had left on wing and silent foot at the approach of winter. As flock after flock of the birds returned and he recognized the old echoes reawakening, he found to his surprise that he had been lonely for them and was hailing their return with great joy. All his fears were forgotten. Instead, he was possessed of an overpowering desire to know what they were, to learn where they had been, and whether they would make friends with him as the winter birds had done; and if they did, would they be as fickle? For, with the running sap, creeping worm, and winging bug, most of Freckles' "chickens" had deserted him, entered the swamp, and feasted to such a state of plethora on its store that they cared little for his supply, so that in the strenuous days of mating and nest-building the boy was deserted.

He chafed at the birds' ingratitude, but he found speedy consolation in watching and befriending the new-comers. He surely would have been proud and highly pleased if he had known that many of the former inhabitants of the interior swamp now grouped their nests beside the timber-line solely for the sake of his protection and company.

The yearly resurrection of the Limberlost is a mighty revival. Freckles stood back and watched with awe and envy the gradual reclothing and repopulation of the swamp. Keen-eyed and alert through danger and loneliness, he noted every stage of development, from the first piping frog and unsheathing bud, to full leafage and the return of the last migrant.

The knowledge of his complete loneliness and utter insignificance was hourly thrust upon him. He brooded and fretted until he was in a fever; yet he never guessed the cause. He was filled with a vast impatience, a longing that he scarcely could endure.

It was June by the zodiac, June by the Limberlost, and by every delight of a newly resurrected season it should have been June in the hearts of all men. Yet Freckles scowled darkly as he came down the trail, and the running *tap, tap* that tested the sagging wire and telegraphed word of his coming to his furred and feathered friends of the swamp, this morning carried the story of his discontent a mile ahead of him.

Freckles' special pet, a dainty, yellow-coated, black-sleeved, cock goldfinch, had remained on the wire for several days past the bravest of all; and Freckles, absorbed with the cunning and beauty of the tiny fellow, never guessed that he was being duped. For the goldfinch was skipping, flirting, and swinging for the express purpose of so holding his attention that he would not look up and see a small cradle of thistledown and wool perilously near his head. In the beginning of brooding, the spunky little homesteader had clung heroically to the wire when he was almost paralyzed with fright. When day after day passed and brought only softly whistled repetitions of his call, a handful of crumbs on the top of a locust line-post, and gently worded coaxings, he grew in confidence. Of late he had sung and swung during the passing of Freckles, who, not dreaming of the nest and the solemn-eyed little hen so close above, thought himself unusually gifted in his power to attract the birds. This morning the goldfinch scarcely could believe his ears, and clung to the wire until an unusually vicious rap sent him spinning a foot in air, and his "*Ptseet*" came with a squall of utter panic.

The wires were ringing with a story the birds could not translate, and Freckles was quite as ignorant of the trouble as they.

A peculiar movement beneath a small walnut-tree

caught his attention. He stopped to investigate. There was an unusually large Luna cocoon, and the moth was bursting the upper end in its struggles to reach light and air. Freckles stood and stared.

"There's something in there trying to get out," he muttered. "Wonder if I could help it? Guess I best not be trying. If I hadn't happened along, there wouldn't have been any one to do anything, and maybe I'd only be hurting it. It's—it's—— Oh, skaggany! It's just being born!"

Freckles gasped with surprise. The moth cleared the opening, and with many wabblings and contortions climbed up the tree. He stared speechless with amazement as the moth crept around a limb and clung to the under side. There was a big pursy body, almost as large as his thumb, and of the very snowiest white that Freckles ever had seen. There was a band of delicate lavender across its forehead, and its feet were of the same colour; there were antlers, like tiny, straw-coloured ferns, on its head, and from its shoulders hung the crumpled wet wings. As Freckles gazed, tense with astonishment, he saw that these were expanding, drooping, taking on colour, and small, oval markings were beginning to show.

The minutes passed. Freckles' steady gaze never wavered. Without realizing it, he was trembling with eagerness and anxiety. As he saw what was taking place, "It's going to fly," he breathed in hushed wonder. The morning sun fell on the moth and dried its velvet down, while the warm air made it fluffy. The rapidly growing wings began to show the most delicate green, with lavender fore-ribs, transparent, eye-shaped markings, edged with lines of red, tan, and black, and long, crisp trailers.

Freckles was whispering to himself for fear of disturbing the moth. It began a systematic exercise of raising and lowering its exquisite wings to dry them and to establish circulation. The boy realized that soon it would be able to spread them and sail away. His long-coming soul sent up its first shivering cry.

"I don't know what it is! Oh, I wish I knew! How I wish I knew! It must be something grand! It can't be a butterfly! It's away too big. Oh, I wish there was some one to tell me what it is!"

He climbed on the locust post, and balancing himself with the wire, held a finger in the line of the moth's advance up the twig. It unhesitatingly climbed on, so he stepped to the path, holding it to the light and examining it closely. Then he held it in the shade and turned it, gloating over its markings and beautiful colouring. When he held the moth to the limb, it climbed on, still waving those magnificent wings.

"My, but I'd like to be staying with you!" he said. "But if I was to stand here all day you couldn't grow any prettier than you are right now, and I wouldn't grow smart enough to tell what you are. I suppose there's some one who knows. Of course there is! Mr. McLean said there were people who knew every leaf, bird, and flower in the Limberlost. Oh Lord! How I wish You'd be telling me just this one thing!"

The goldfinch had ventured back to the wire, for there was his mate, only a few inches above the man-creature's head; and indeed, he simply must not be allowed to look up, so the brave little fellow rocked on the wire and piped, as he had done every day for a week: "*See me? See me?*"

"See you! Of course I see you," growled Freckles. "I see you day after day, and what good is it doing me? I might see you every morning for a year, and then not be able to be telling any one about it. 'Seen a bird with black silk wings—little, and yellow as any canary.' That's as far as I'd get. What you doing here, anyway? Have you a mate? What's your name? 'See you?' I reckon I see you; but I might as well be blind, for any good it's doing me!"

Freckles impatiently struck the wire. With a screech of fear, the goldfinch fled precipitately. His mate arose from the nest with a whirr—Freckles looked up and saw it.

"O-ho!" he cried. "So *that's* what you are doing here! You have a wife. And so close my head I have been mighty near wearing a bird on my bonnet, and never knew it!"

Freckles laughed at his own jest, while in better humour he climbed to examine the neat, tiny cradle and its contents. The hen darted at him in a frenzy. "Now, where do you come in?" he demanded, when he saw that she was not similar to the goldfinch.

"You be clearing out of here! This is none of your fry. This is the nest of me little, yellow friend of the wire, and you shan't be touching it. Don't blame you for wanting to see, though. My, but it's a fine nest and beauties of eggs. Will you be keeping away, or will I fire this stick at you?"

Freckles dropped to the trail. The hen darted to the nest and settled on it with a tender, coddling movement. He of the yellow coat flew to the edge to make sure that everything was right. It would have been plain to the veriest novice that they were partners in that cradle.

"Well, I'll be switched!" muttered Freckles. "If that ain't both their nest! And he's yellow and she's green, or she's yellow and he's green. Of course, I don't know, and I haven't any way to find out, but it's plain as the nose on your face that they are both ready to be fighting for that nest, so, of course, they belong. Doesn't that beat you? Say, that's what's been sticking me all of this week on that grass-nest in the thorn-tree down the line. One day a blue bird is setting, so I think it is hers. The next day a brown bird is on, and I chase it off because the nest is blue's. Next day the brown bird is on again, and I let her be, because I think it must be hers. Next day, be golly, blue's on, and off I send her because it's brown's; and now, I bet my hat, it's both their nest, and I've only been bothering them and making a big fool of mesilf. Pretty specimen I am, pretending to be a friend to the birds, and so blamed ignorant I don't know which ones go in pairs, and blue and brown are a pair, of course, if yellow and green are—and there's the red birds! I never thought of them! He's red and she's gray—and now I want to be knowing, are they all different? Why no! Of course, they ain't! There's the jays all blue, and the crows all black."

The tide of Freckles' discontent welled until he almost choked with anger and chagrin. He plodded down the trail, scowling blackly and viciously spanging the wire.

At the finches' nest he left the line and peered into the thorn-tree. There was no bird brooding. He pressed closer to take a peep at the snowy, spotless little eggs he had found so beautiful, when at the slight noise up raised four tiny baby heads with wide-open mouths, uttering hunger cries. Freckles stepped back. The brown bird alighted on the edge and closed one cavity with a wiggling green worm, while not two minutes later the blue filled another with a white. That settled it. The blue and brown were mates. Once again Freckles repeated his: "How I wish I knew!"

Around the bridge spanning Sleepy Snake Creek the swale spread widely, the timber was scattering, and willows, rushes, marsh-grass, and splendid wild flowers grew abundantly. Here lazy, big, black water-snakes, for which the creek was named, sunned on the bushes, wild ducks and grebe chattered, cranes and herons fished, and muskrats ploughed the bank in queer, rolling furrows. It was always a place full of interest, so Freckles loved to linger on the bridge, watching the marsh and water people. He also transacted affairs of importance with the wild flowers and sweet marsh-grass. He enjoyed splashing through the shallow pools on either side of the bridge.

Then, too, where the creek entered the swamp was a place of unusual beauty. The water spread in darksome, mossy, green pools. Water-plants and lilies grew luxuriantly, throwing up large, rank, green leaves. Nowhere else in the Limberlost could be found frog-music to equal that of the mouth of the creek. The drumming and piping rolled in never-ending orchestral effect, while the full chorus rang to its accompaniment throughout the season.

Freckles slowly followed the path leading from the bridge to the line. It was the one spot at which he might relax his vigilance. The boldest timber thief the swamp ever had known would not have attempted to enter it by the mouth of the creek, on account of the water and because there was no protection from surrounding trees. He was bending the rank grass with his cudgel, and thinking of the shade the denser swamp afforded, when he suddenly dodged sidewise; the cudgel whistled sharply through the air and Freckles sprang back.

From the clear sky above him, first level with his face, then skimming, dipping, tilting, whirling until it struck, quill down, in the path in front of him, came a glossy, iridescent, big black feather. As it touched the ground, Freckles snatched it up with almost a continuous movement facing the sky. There was not a tree of any size in a large open space. There was no wind to carry it. From the clear sky it had fallen, and Freckles, gazing eagerly into the arch of June blue with a few lazy clouds floating high in the sea of ether, had neither mind nor knowledge to dream of a bird hanging as if frozen there. He turned the big quill questioningly, and again his awed eyes swept the sky.

"A feather dropped from Heaven!" he breathed reverently. "Are the holy angels moulting? But no; if they were, it would be white. Maybe all the angels are not for being white. What if the angels of God are white and those of the devil are black? But a black one has no business up there. Maybe some poor black angel is so tired of being punished it's for slipping to the gates, beating its wings trying to make the Master hear!"

Again and again Freckles searched the sky, but there was no answering gleam of golden gates, no form of sailing bird; then he went slowly on his way, turning the feather and wondering about it. It was a wing quill, eighteen inches in length, with a heavy spine, gray at the base, shading to jet black at the tip, and it caught the play of the sun's rays in slanting gleams of green and bronze. Again Freckles' "old man of the sea" sat sullen and heavy on his shoulders and weighted him down until his step lagged and his heart ached.

"Where did it come from? What is it? Oh, how I wish I knew!" he kept repeating as he turned and studied the feather, with almost unseeing eyes, so intently was he thinking.

Before him spread a large, green pool, filled with rotting logs and leaves, bordered with delicate ferns and grasses among which lifted the creamy spikes of the arrow-head, the blue of water-hyacinth, and the delicate yellow of the jewel-flower. As Freckles leaned, handling the feather and staring at it, then into the depths of the pool, he once more gave voice to his old query: "I wonder what it is!"

Straight across from him, couched in the mosses of a soggy old log, a big green bullfrog, with palpitant throat and batting eyes, lifted his head and bellowed in answer: "*Fin' dout! Fin' dout!*"

"Wha—what's that?" stammered Freckles, almost too much bewildered to speak. "I—I know you are only a bullfrog, but, be jabbers, that sounded mightily like speech. Wouldn't you please to be saying it over?"

The bullfrog cuddled contentedly in the ooze. Then suddenly he lifted his voice, and, as an imperative drum-beat, rolled it again: "*Fin' dout! Fin' dout! Find out!*"

Freckles had the answer. Something seemed to snap in his brain. There was a wavering flame before his eyes. Then his mind cleared. His head lifted in a new poise, his shoulders squared, while his spine straightened. The agony was over. His soul floated free. Freckles came into his birthright.

"Before God, I will!" He uttered the oath so impressively that the recording angel never winced as he posted it in the prayer column.

Freckles set his hat over the top of one of the locust posts used between trees to hold up the wire while he fastened the feather securely in the band. Then he started down the line, talking to himself as men who have worked long alone always fall into the habit of doing.

"What a fool I have been!" he muttered. "Of course that's what I have to do! There wouldn't likely anybody be doing it for me. Of course I can! What am I a man for? If I was a four-footed thing of the swamp, maybe I couldn't; but a man can do anything if he's the grit to work hard enough and stick at it, Mr. McLean is always saying, and here's the way I am to do it. He said, too, that there were people that knew everything in the swamp. Of course they have written books! The thing for me to be doing is to quit moping and be buying some. Never bought a book in me life, or anything else of much account, for that matter. Oh, ain't I glad I didn't waste me money! I'll surely be having enough to get a few. Let me see."

Freckles sat on a log, took his pencil and account-book, and figured on a back page. He had walked the timber-line ten months. His pay was thirty dollars a month, and his board cost him eight. That left twenty-two dollars a month, and his clothing had cost him very little. At the least he had two hundred dollars in the bank. He drew a deep breath and smiled at the sky with satisfaction.

"I'll be having a book about all the birds, trees, flowers, butterflies, and—— Yes, by gummy! I'll be having one about the frogs—if it takes every cent I have," he promised himself.

He put away the account-book, that was his most cherished possession, caught up his stick, and started down the line. The even tap, tap, and the cheery, gladsome whistle carried far ahead of him the message that Freckles was himself again.

He fell into a rapid pace, for he had lost time that morning, when he rounded the last curve he was almost running. There was a chance that the Boss might be there for his weekly report.

Then, wavering, flickering, darting here and there over the sweet marsh-grass, came a large black shadow, sweeping so closely before him that for the second time that morning Freckles dodged and sprang back. He had seen some owls and hawks of the swamp that he thought might be classed as large birds, but never anything like this, for six feet it spread its big, shining wings. Its strong feet could be seen drawn among its feathers. The sun glinted on its sharp, hooked beak. Its eyes glowed, caught the light, and seemed able to pierce the ground at his feet. It cared no more for Freckles than if he had not been there; for it perched on a low tree, while a second later it awkwardly hopped to the trunk of a lightning-riven elm, turned its back, and began searching the blue.

Freckles looked just in time to see a second shadow sweep the grass; and another bird, a trifle smaller and not quite so brilliant in the light, slowly sailed down to perch beside the first. Evidently they were mates, for with a queer, rolling hop the first-comer shivered his bronze wings, sidled to the new arrival, and gave her a silly little peck on her wing. Then he coquettishly drew away and ogled her. He lifted his head, waddled from her a few steps, awkwardly ambled back, and gave her such a simple sort of kiss on her beak that Freckles burst into a laugh, but clapped his hand over his mouth to stifle the sound.

The lover ducked and side-stepped a few feet. He spread his wings and slowly and softly waved them precisely as if he were fanning his charmer, which was indeed the result he accomplished. Then a wave of uncontrollable tenderness moved him so he hobbled to his bombardment once more. He faced her squarely this time, and turned his head from side to side with queer little jerks and indiscriminate peckings at her wings and head, and smirkings that really should have been irresistible. She yawned and shuffled away indifferently. Freckles reached up, pulled the quill from his hat, and looking from it to the birds, nodded in settled conviction.

"So you're me black angels, ye spalpeens! No wonder

you didn't get in! But I'll back you to come closer it than any other birds ever did. You fly higher than I can see. Have you picked the Limberlost for a good thing and come to try it? Well, you can be me chickens if you want to, but I'm blest if you ain't cool for new ones. Why don't you take this stick for a gun and go skinning a mile?"

Freckles broke into an unrestrained laugh, for the bird-lover was keen about his courting, while evidently his mate was diffident. When he approached too boisterously, she relieved him of a goodly tuft of feathers and sent him backward in a series of squirmy little jumps that gave the boy an idea of what had happened up-sky to send the falling feather across his pathway.

"Score one for the lady! I'll be umpiring this," volunteered Freckles.

With a ravishing swagger, half-lifted wings, and deep, guttural hissing, the lover approached again. He suddenly lifted his body, but she coolly rocked forward on the limb, glided gracefully beneath him, and slowly sailed into the Limberlost. He recovered himself and gazed after her in astonishment.

Freckles hurried down the trail, shaking with laughter. When he neared the path to the clearing and saw the Boss sitting motionless on the mare that was the pride of his heart, the boy broke into a run.

"Oh, Mr. McLean!" he cried. "I hope I haven't kept you waiting very long! And the sun is getting hot! I have been so slow this morning! I could have gone faster, only there were that many things to keep me, and I didn't know you would be here. I'll hurry after this. I've never had to be giving excuses before. The line wasn't down, and there wasn't a sign of trouble; it was other things that were making me late."

McLean, smiling on the boy, immediately noticed the difference in him. This flushed, panting, talkative lad was not the same creature who had sought him in despair and bitterness. He watched in wonder as Freckles mopped the perspiration from his forehead and began to laugh. Then, forgetting all his customary reserve with the Boss, the pent-up boyishness in the lad broke forth. With an eloquence of which he never dreamed he told his story. He talked with such enthusiasm that McLean never took his eyes from his face or shifted in the saddle until he described the strange bird-lover, and then the Boss suddenly bent over the pommel and laughed with the boy.

Freckles decorated his story with keen appreciation and rare touches of Irish wit and drollery that made it most interesting as well as very funny. It was a first attempt at descriptive narration. With an inborn gift for striking the vital point, a naturalist's dawning enthusiasm for the wonders of the Limberlost, and the welling joy of his newly found happiness, he made McLean see the struggles of the moth and its freshly painted wings, the dainty, brilliant bird-mates of different colours, the feather sliding through the clear air, the palpitant throat and batting eyes of the frog; while his version of the big bird's courtship won for the Boss the best laugh he had enjoyed for years.

"They're in the middle of the swamp now," said Freckles. "Do you suppose there is any chance of them staying with me chickens? If they do, they'll be about the queerest I have; but I tell you, sir, I am finding some plum good ones. There's a new kind over at the mouth of the creek that uses its wings like feet and walks on all fours. It travels like a thrashing machine. There's another, tall as me waist, with a bill a foot long, a neck near two, not the thickness of me wrist and an elegant colour. He's some blue and gray, touched up with black, white, and brown. The voice of him is such that if he'd be going up and standing beside a tree and crying at it a few times he could be sawing it square off. I don't know but it would be a good idea to try him on the gang, sir."

McLean laughed. "Those must be blue herons, Freckles," he said. "And it doesn't seem possible, but your description of the big black birds sounds like genuine black vultures. They are common enough in the South. I've seen them numerous around the lumber-camps of Georgia, but I never before heard of any this far north. They must be strays. You have described perfectly our nearest equivalent to a branch of these birds called in Europe Pharaoh's chickens, but if they are coming to the Limberlost they will have to drop Pharaoh and become Freckles' chickens, like the remainder of the birds; won't they? Or are they too odd and ugly to interest you?"

"Oh, not at all, at all!" cried Freckles, bursting into pure brogue in his haste. "I don't know as I'd be calling them exactly pretty, and they do move like a rocking-horse loping, but they are so big and fearless. They have a fine colour for black birds, and their feet and beaks seem so strong. You never saw anything so keen as their eyes!

And fly? Why, just think, sir, they must be flying miles straight up, for they were out of sight completely when the feather fell. I don't suppose I've a chicken in the swamp that can go as close heaven as those big, black fellows, and then——"

Freckles' voice dragged and he hesitated.

"Then what?" interestedly urged McLean.

"He was loving her so," answered Freckles in a hushed voice. "I know it looked awful funny, and I laughed and told on him, but if I'd taken time to think I don't believe I'd have done it. You see, I've seen such a little bit of loving in me life. You easily can be understanding that at the Home it was every day the old story of neglect and desertion. Always people that didn't even care enough for their children to keep them, so you see, sir, I had to like him for trying so hard to make her know how he loved her. Of course, they're only birds, but if they are caring for each other like that, why, it's just the same as people, ain't it?"

Freckles lifted his brave, steady eyes to the Boss.

"If anybody loved me like that, Mr. McLean, I wouldn't be spending any time on how they looked or moved. All I'd be thinking of would be how they felt toward me. If they will stay, I'll be caring as much for them as any chickens I have. If I did laugh at them I thought he was just fine!"

The face of McLean was a study; but the honest eyes of the boy were so compelling that he found himself answering: "You are right, Freckles. He's a gentleman, isn't he? And the only real chicken you have. Of course he'll remain! The Limberlost will be paradise for his family.

And now, Freckles, what has been the trouble all spring? You have done your work as faithfully as any one could ask, but I can't help seeing that there is something wrong. Are you tired of your job?"

"I love it," answered Freckles. "It will almost break me heart when the gang comes and begins tearing up the swamp and scaring away me chickens."

"Then what is the trouble?" insisted McLean.

"I think, sir, it's been books," answered Freckles. "You see, I didn't realize it meself until the bullfrog told me this morning. I hadn't ever even heard about a place like this. Anyway, I wasn't understanding how it would be, if I had. Being among these beautiful things every day, I got so anxious like to be knowing and naming them, that it got to eating into me and went and made me near sick, when I was well as I could be. Of course, I learned to read, write, and figure some at school, but there was nothing there, or in any of the city that I ever got to see, that would make a fellow even be dreaming of such interesting things as there are here. I've seen the parks—but good Lord, they ain't even beginning to be in it with the Limberlost! It's all new and strange to me. I don't know a thing about any of it. The bullfrog told me to '*find out,*' plain as day, and books are the only way; ain't they?"

"Of course," said McLean, astonished at himself for his heartfelt relief. He had not guessed until that minute what it would have meant to him to have Freckles give up. "You know enough to study out what you want yourself, if you have the books; don't you?"

"I am pretty sure I do," said Freckles. "I learned all

I'd the chance at in the Home, and me schooling was good as far as it went. Wouldn't let you go past fourteen, you know. I always did me sums perfect, and loved me history-books. I had them almost by heart. I never could get me grammar to suit them. They said it was just born in me to go wrong talking, and if it hadn't been I suppose I would have picked it up from the other children; but I'd the best voice of any of them in the Home or at school. I could knock them all out singing. I was always leader in the Home, and once one of the superintendents gave me car-fare and let me go into the city and sing in a boys' choir. The master said I'd the swatest voice of them all until it got rough like, and then he made me quit for awhile, but he said it would be coming back by now, and I'm railly thinking it is, sir, for I've tried on the line a bit of late and it seems to go smooth again and lots stronger. That and me chickens have been all the company I've been having, and it will be all I'll want if I can have some books and learn the real names of things, where they come from, and why they do such interesting things. It's been fretting me more than I knew to be shut up here among all these wonders and not knowing a thing. I wanted to ask you what some books would cost me, and if you'd be having the goodness to get me the right ones. I think I have enough money."

Freckles offered his account-book and the Boss studied it gravely.

"You needn't touch your account, Freckles," he said. "Ten dollars from this month's pay will provide you everything you need to start on. I will write a friend in Grand

Rapids to-day to select you the very best and send them at once."

Freckles' eyes were shining.

"Never owned a book in me life!" he said. "Even me school-books were never mine. Lord! How I used to wish I could have just one of them for me very own! Won't it be fun to see me saw-bird and me little yellow fellow looking at me from the pages of a book, and their real names and all about them printed alongside? How long will it be taking, sir?"

"Ten days should do it nicely," said McLean. Then, seeing Freckles' lengthening face, he added: "I'll have Duncan bring you a ten-bushel store-box the next time he goes to town. He can haul it to the west entrance and set it up wherever you want it. You can put in your spare time filling it with the specimens you find until the books come, and then you can study out what you have. I suspect you could collect specimens that I could send to naturalists in the city and sell for you; things like that winged creature, this morning. I don't know much in that line, but it must have been a moth, and it might have been rare. I've seen them by the thousand in museums, and in all nature I don't remember rarer colouring than their wings. I'll order you a butterfly-net and box and show you how scientists pin specimens. Possibly you can make a fine collection of these swamp beauties. It will be all right for you to take a pair of different moths and butterflies, but I don't want to hear of your killing any birds. They are protected by heavy fines."

McLean rode away leaving Freckles staring aghast.

Then he saw the point and smiled. Standing on the trail, he twirled the feather and thought over the morning.

"Well, if life ain't getting to be worth living!" he said wonderingly. "Biggest streak of luck I ever had! 'Bout time something was coming my way, but I wouldn't ever thought anybody could strike such magnificent prospects through only a falling feather."

CHAPTER IV

Wherein Freckles Faces Trouble Bravely and Opens the Way For New Experiences

CHAPTER IV

Wherein Freckles Faces Trouble Bravely and Opens the Way For New Experiences

ON DUNCAN'S return from his next trip to town there was a big store-box loaded on the back of his wagon. He drove to the west entrance of the swamp, set the box on a stump that Freckles had selected in a beautiful, sheltered place, and made it secure on its foundations with a tree at its back.

"It seems most a pity to nail into that tree," said Duncan. "I haena the time to examine into the grain of it, but it looks as if it might be a rare ane. Anyhow, the nailin' winna hurt it deep, and havin' the case by it will make it safer if it is a guid ane."

"Isn't it an oak?" asked Freckles.

"Ay," said Duncan. "It looks like it might be ane of thae fine-grained white anes that mak' such grand furniture."

When the body of the case was secure, Duncan made a door from the lid and fastened it with hinges. He drove a staple, screwed on a latch, and gave Freckles a small padlock—so that he might fasten in his treasures safely. He made a shelf at the top for his books, and last of all covered the case with oil-cloth.

It was the first time in Freckles' life that any one ever

had done that much for his pleasure, and it warmed his heart with pure joy. If the interior of the box already had been covered with the rarest treasures of the Limberlost he could have been no happier.

When the big teamster stood back to look at his work he laughingly quoted, "'Neat, but no' gaudy,' as McLean says. All we're needing now is a coat of paint to make a cupboard that would turn Sarah green with envy. Ye'll find that safe an' dry, lad, an' that's all that's needed."

"Mr. Duncan," said Freckles, "I don't know why you are being so mighty good to me; but if you have any jobs at the cabin that I could do for you or Mrs. Duncan, hours off the line, it would make me mighty happy."

Duncan laughed. "Ye needna feel ye are obliged to me, lad. Ye mauna think I could take a half-day off in the best hauling season and go to town for boxes to rig up, and spend of my little for fixtures."

"I knew Mr. McLean sent you," said Freckles, his eyes wide and bright with happiness. "It's so good of him. How I wish I could do something that would please him as much!"

"Why, Freckles," said Duncan, as he knelt and began collecting his tools, "I canna see that it will hurt ye to be told that ye are doing every day a thing that pleases the Boss as much as anything ye could do. Ye're being uncommon faithful, lad, and honest as old Father Time. McLean is trusting ye as he would his own flesh and blood."

"Oh, Duncan!" cried the happy boy. "Are you sure?"

"Why I know," answered Duncan. "I wadna venture to say so else. In those first days he cautioned me na to tell ye, but now he wadna care. D'ye ken, Freckles, that some of the single trees ye are guarding are worth a thousand dollars?"

Freckles caught his breath and stood speechless.

"Ye see," said Duncan, "that's why they maun be watched so closely. They tak', say, for instance, a burl maple—bird's eye they call it in the factory, because it's full o' wee knots and twists that look like the eye of a bird. They saw it out in sheets no muckle thicker than writin'-paper. Then they make up the furniture out of cheaper wood and cover it with the maple—veneer, they call it. When it's all done and polished ye never saw onythin' grander. Gang into a retail shop the next time ye are in town and see some. By sawin' it thin that way they get finish for thousands of dollars' worth of furniture from a single tree. If ye dinna watch faithful, and Black Jack gets out a few he has marked, it means the loss of more money than ye ever dreamed of, lad. The other night, down at camp, some son of Balaam was suggestin' that ye might be sellin' the Boss out to Jack and lettin' him tak' the trees secretly, and nobody wad ever ken till the gang gets here."

A wave of scarlet flooded Freckles' face and he blazed hotly at the insult.

"And the Boss," continued Duncan, coolly ignoring Freckles' anger, "he lays back just as cool as cowcumbers an' says: 'I'll give a thousand dollars to ony man that will show me a fresh stump when we reach the Limberlost,' says he. Some of the men just snapped him up that they'd find some. So you see how the Boss is trustin' ye, lad."

"I am gladder than I can ever expriss," said Freckles.

"And now will I be walking double time to keep some of them from cutting a tree to get all that money!"

"Mither o' Moses!" howled Duncan. "Ye can trust the Scotch to bungle things a'thegither. McLean was only meanin' to show ye all confidence and honour. He's gone and set a high price for some dirty whelp to ruin ye. I was just tryin' to show ye how he felt toward ye, and I've gone an' give ye that worry to bear. Damn the Scotch! They're so slow an' so dumb!"

"Exciptin' prisint company?" sweetly inquired Freckles.

"No!" growled Duncan. "Headin' the list! He'd nae business to set a price on ye, lad, for that's about the amount of it, an' I'd nae right to tell ye. We've both done ye ill, an' both meanin' the verra best. Juist what I'm always sayin' to Sarah."

"I am mighty proud of what you have been telling me, Duncan," said Freckles. "I need the warning, sure. For with the books coming I might be timpted to neglect me work when double watching is needed. Thank you more than I can say for putting me on to it. What you've told me may be the saving of me. I won't stop for dinner now. I'll be getting along the east line, and when I come around about three, maybe Mother Duncan will let me have a glass of milk and a bite of something."

"Ye see now!" cried Duncan in disgust. "Ye'll start on that seven-mile tramp with na bite to stay your stomach. What was it I told ye?"

"You told me that the Scotch had the hardest heads and the softest hearts of any people that's living," answered Freckles.

Duncan grunted in gratified disapproval.

Freckles picked up his club and started down the line, whistling cheerily, for he had an unusually long repertoire upon which to draw.

Duncan went straight to the lower camp, and calling McLean aside, repeated the conversation verbatim, ending: "And nae matter what happens now or ever, dinna ye dare let onythin' make ye believe that Freckles hasna guarded faithful as ony man could."

"I don't think anything could shake my faith in the lad," answered McLean.

Freckles was whistling merrily. He kept one eye religiously on the line. The other he divided between the path, his friends of the wire, and a search of the sky for his latest arrivals. Every day since their coming he had seen them, either hanging as small, black clouds above the swamp or bobbing over logs and trees with their queer, tilting walk. Whenever he could spare time, he entered the swamp and tried to make friends with them, for they were the tamest of all his unnumbered subjects. They ducked, dodged, and ambled around him, over logs and bushes, and not even a near approach would drive them to flight.

For two weeks he had found them circling over the Limberlost regularly, but one morning the female was missing and only the big black chicken hung sentinel above the swamp. His mate did not reappear in the following days, and Freckles grew very anxious. He spoke of it to Mrs. Duncan, and she quieted his fears by raising a delightful hope in their stead.

"Why, Freckles, if it's the hen-bird ye are missing, it's

ten to one she's safe," she said. "She's laid, and is setting, ye silly! Watch him and mark whaur he lichts. Then follow and find the nest. Some Sabbath we'll all gang see it."

Accepting this theory, Freckles began searching for the nest. Because these "chickens" were large, as the hawks, he looked among the tree-tops until he almost sprained the back of his neck. He had half the crow and hawk nests in the swamp located. He searched for this nest instead of collecting subjects for his case. He found the pair the middle of one forenoon on the elm where he had watched their love-making. The big black chicken was feeding his mate; so it was proved that they were a pair, they were both alive, and undoubtedly she was brooding. After that Freckles' nest-hunting continued with renewed zeal, but as he had no idea where to look and Duncan could offer no helpful suggestion, the nest was no nearer to being found.

Coming from a long day on the trail, Freckles saw Duncan's children awaiting him much closer the swale than they usually ventured, and from their wild gestures he knew that something had happened. He began to run, but the cry that reached him was: "The books have come!"

How they hurried! Freckles lifted the youngest to his shoulder, the second took his club and dinner-pail, and when they reached Mrs. Duncan they found her at work on a big box. She had loosened the lid, and then she laughingly sat on it.

"Ye canna have a peep in here until ye have washed

and eaten supper," she said. "It's all ready on the table. Ance ye begin on this, ye'll no be willin' to tak' your nose o' it till bedtime, and I willna get my work done the nicht. We've eaten long ago."

It was difficult work, but Freckles smiled bravely. He made himself neat, swallowed a few bites, then came so eagerly that Mrs. Duncan yielded, although she said she very well knew all the time that his supper would be spoiled.

Lifting the lid, they removed the packing and found in that box books on birds, trees, flowers, moths, and butterflies. There was also one containing Freckles' bullfrog, true to life. Besides these were a butterfly-net, a naturalist's tin specimen-box, a bottle of cyanide, a box of cotton, a paper of long, steel specimen-pins, and a letter telling what all these things were and how to use them.

At the discovery of each new treasure, Freckles shouted: "Will you be looking at this, now?"

Mrs. Duncan cried: "Weel, I be drawed on!"

The eldest boy turned a somersault for every extra, while the baby, trying to follow his example, bunched over in a sidewise sprawl and cut his foot on the axe with which his mother had prized up the box-lid. That sobered them, they carried the books indoors. Mrs. Duncan had a top shelf in her closet cleared for them, far above the reach of meddling little fingers.

When Freckles started for the trail next morning, the shining new specimen-box flashed on his back. The black "chicken," a mere speck in the blue, caught the gleam of it. The folded net hung beside the boy's hatchet, and the bird-book was in the box. He walked the line and tested each section scrupulously, watching every foot of the trail, for he was determined not to slight his work; but if ever a boy "made haste slowly" in a hurry, it was Freckles that morning. When at last he reached the space he had cleared and planted around his case, his heart swelled with the pride of possessing even so much that he could call his own, while his quick eyes feasted on the beauty of it.

He had made a large room with the door of the case set even with one side of it. On three sides, fine big bushes of wild-rose climbed to the lower branches of the trees. Part of his walls were mallow, part alder, thorn, willow, and dogwood. Below there filled in a solid mass of pale pink sheep-laurel, and yellow St. John's wort, while the amber threads of the dodder interlaced everywhere. At one side the swamp came close, here cat-tails grew in profusion. In front of them he had planted a row of water-hyacinths without disturbing in the least the state of their azure bloom, and where the ground arose higher for his floor, a row of foxfire, that soon would be open.

To the left he had discovered a queer natural arrangement of the trees, that grew to giant size and were set in a gradually narrowing space so that a long, open vista stretched away until lost in the dim recesses of the swamp. A little trimming of underbush, rolling of dead logs, levelling of floor and carpeting with moss, made it easy to understand why Freckles had named this the "cathedral"; yet he never had been taught that "the groves were God's first temples."

On either side of the trees that constituted the first

arch of this dim vista of the swamp he planted ferns that grew waist-high thus early in the season, and so skilfully the work had been done that not a frond drooped because of the change. Opposite, he cleared a space and made a flower-bed. He filled one end with every delicate, lacy vine and fern he could transplant successfully. The body of the bed was a riot of colour. Here he set growing dainty blue-eyed-Marys and blue-eyed grass side by side. He planted harebells; violets, blue, white, and yellow; wild geranium, cardinal-flower, columbine, pink snake's mouth, buttercups, painted trilliums, and orchis. Here were blood-root, moccasin-flower, hepatica, pitcher-plant, Jack-in-the-pulpit, and every other flower of the Limberlost that was in bloom or bore a bud presaging a flower. Every day saw the addition of new specimens. The place would have driven a botanist wild with envy.

On the line side he left the bushes thick for concealment, entering by a narrow path he and Duncan had cleared in setting up the case. He called this the front door, though he used every precaution to hide it. He built rustic seats between several of the trees, levelled the floor, and thickly carpeted it with rank, heavy, woolly-dog moss. Around the case he planted wild clematis, bitter-sweet, and wild grape-vines, and trained them over it until it was almost covered. Every day he planted new flowers, cut back rough bushes, and coaxed out graceful ones. His pride in his room was very great, but he had no idea how surprisingly beautiful it would appear to any one who had not witnessed its growth and construction.

This morning Freckles walked straight to his case, unlocked it, and set his apparatus and dinner inside. He planted a new specimen he had found close the trail, and, bringing his old scrap-bucket from the corner in which it was hidden, from a near-by pool he dipped water to pour over his carpet and flowers.

Then he took out the bird-book, settled comfortably on a bench, and with a deep sigh of satisfaction turned to the section headed "V." Past "veery" and "vireo" he went, down the line until his finger, trembling with eagerness, stopped at "vulture."

"'Great black California vulture,'" he read.

"Humph! This side the Rockies will do for us."

"'Common turkey-buzzard.'"

"Well, we ain't hunting common turkeys. McLean said chickens, and what he says goes."

"'Black vulture of the South.'"

"Here we are arrived at once."

Freckles' finger followed the line, and he read scraps aloud.

"'Common in the South. Sometimes called Jim Crow. Nearest equivalent to C-a-t-h-a-r-t-e-s A-t-r-a-t-a.'"

"How the divil am I ever to learn them corkin' big words by mesel'?"

"'—the Pharaoh's Chickens of European species. Sometimes stray north as far as Virginia and Kentucky——'"

"And sometimes farther," interpolated Freckles, "'cos I got them right here in Indiana so like these pictures I can just see me big chicken bobbing up to get his ears boxed. Hey?"

"'Light-blue eggs'——"

"Golly! I got to be seeing them!"

"'—big as a common turkey's, but shaped like a hen's, heavily splotched with chocolate——'"

"Caramels, I suppose. And——"

"'—in hollow logs or stumps.'"

"Oh, hagginy! Wasn't I barking up the wrong tree, though? Ought to been looking close the ground all this time. Now it's all to do over, and I suspect the sooner I start the sooner I'll be likely to find them."

Freckles put away his book, dampened the smudge-fire, without which the mosquitoes made the swamp almost unbearable, took his cudgel and lunch, and went to the line. He sat on a log, ate at dinner-time and drank his last drop of water. The heat of June was growing intense. Even on the west of the swamp, where one had full benefit of the breeze from the upland, it was beginning to be unpleasant in the middle of the day.

He brushed the crumbs from his knees and sat resting a while and watching the sky to see if his big chicken were hanging up there. But he came to the earth abruptly, for there were steps coming down the trail that were neither McLean's nor Duncan's—and there never had been others. Freckles' heart leaped hotly. He ran a quick hand over his belt to feel if his revolver and hatchet were there, caught up his cudgel and laid it across his knees—then sat quietly, waiting. Was it Black Jack, or some one even worse? Forced to do something to brace his nerves, he puckered his stiffening lips and began whistling a tune he had led in his clear tenor every year of his life at the Home Christmas exercises.

"Who comes this way, so blithe and gay,
Upon a merry Christmas day?"

His quick Irish wit roused to the ridiculousness of it until he broke into a laugh that steadied him amazingly.

Through the bushes he caught a glimpse of the oncoming figure. His heart flooded with joy, for it was a man from the gang. Wessner had been his bunk-mate the night he came down the corduroy. He knew him as well as any of McLean's men. This was no timber-thief. No doubt the Boss had sent him with a message. Freckles sprang up and called cheerily, a warm welcome on his face.

"Well, it's good telling if you're glad to see me," said Wessner, with something very like a breath of relief. "We been hearing down at the camp you were so mighty touchy you didn't allow a man within a rod of the line."

"No more do I," answered Freckles, "if he's a stranger, but you're from McLean, ain't you?"

"Oh, damn McLean!" said Wessner.

Freckles gripped the cudgel until his knuckles slowly turned purple.

"And are you railly saying so?" he inquired with elaborate politeness.

"Yes, I am," said Wessner. "So would every man of the gang if they wasn't too big cowards to say anything, unless maybe that other slobbering old Scotchman, Duncan. Grinding the lives out of us! Working us like dogs, and paying us starvation wages, while he rolls up his millions and lives like a prince!"

Green lights began to play through the gray of Freckles' eyes.

"Wessner," he said, impressively, "you'd make a fine pattern for the father of liars! Every man on that gang is strong and hilthy, paid all he earns, and treated with the courtesy of a gentleman! As for the Boss living like a prince, he shares fare with you every day of your lives!"

Wessner was not a born diplomat, but he saw he was on the wrong tack, so he tried another.

"How would you like to make a good big pile of money, without even lifting your hand?" he asked.

"Humph!" said Freckles. "Have you been up to Chicago and cornered wheat, and are you offering me a friendly tip on the invistment of me fortune?"

Wessner came close.

"Freckles, old fellow," he said, "if you let me give you a pointer, I can put you on to making a cool five hundred without stepping out of your tracks."

Freckles drew back.

"You needn't be afraid of speaking up," he said. "There isn't a soul in the Limberlost save the birds and the beasts, unless some of your sort's come along and's crowding the privileges of the legal tinints."

"None of *my* friends along," said Wessner. "Nobody knew I came but Black, I—I mean a friend of mine. If you want to hear sense and act with reason, he can see you later, but it ain't necessary. We can make all the plans needed. The trick's so dead small and easy."

"Must be if you have the engineering of it," said Freckles. But he heard, with a sigh of relief, that they were alone.

Wessner was impervious. "You just bet it is! Why, only think, Freckles, slavin' away at a measly little thirty dollars a month, and here is a chance to clear five hundred in a day! You surely won't be the fool to miss it!"

"And how was you proposing for me to stale it?" inquired Freckles. "Or am I just to find it laying in me path beside the line?"

"That's it, Freckles," blustered the Dutchman, "you're just to find it. You needn't do a thing. You needn't know a thing. You name a morning when you will walk up the west side of the swamp and then turn round and walk back down the same side again and the money is yours. Couldn't anything be easier than that, could it?"

"Depinds entirely on the man," said Freckles. The lilt of a lark hanging above the swale beside them was not sweeter than the sweetness of his voice. "To some it would seem to come aisy as breathing; and to some, wringin' the last drop of their heart's blood couldn't force thim! I'm not the man that goes into a scheme like that with the blindfold over me eyes, for, you see, it manes to break trust with the Boss; and I've served him faithful as I knew. You'll have to be making the thing very clear to me understanding."

"It's so dead easy," repeated Wessner, "it makes me tired of the simpleness of it. You see there's a few trees in the swamp that's real gold-mines. There's three especial. Two are back in, but one's square on the line.

Why, your pottering old Scotch fool of a Boss nailed the wire to it with his own hands! He never noticed where the bark had been peeled, or saw what it was. If you will stay on this side of the trail just one day we can have it cut, loaded, and ready to drive out at night. Next morning you can find it, report, and be the busiest man in the search for us. We know where to fix it all safe and easy. Then McLean has a bet up with a couple of the gang that there can't be a raw stump found in the Limberlost. There's plenty of witnesses to swear to it, and I know three that will. There's a cool thousand, and this tree is worth all of that, raw. Say, it's a gold-mine, I tell you, and just five hundred of it is yours. There's no danger on earth to you, for you've got McLean that bamboozled you could sell out the whole swamp and he'd never mistrust you. What do you say?"

Freckles' soul was satisfied. "Is that all?" he asked.

"No, it ain't," said Wessner. "If you really want to brace up and be a man and go into the thing for keeps, you can make five times that in a week. My friend knows a dozen others we could get out in a few days, and all you'd have to do would be to keep out of sight. Then you could take your money and skip some night, and begin life like a gentleman somewhere else. What do you think about it?"

Freckles purred like a kitten.

"'Twould be a rare joke on the Boss," he said, "to be stalin' from him the very thing he's trusted me to guard, and be getting me wages all winter throwed in free. And you're making the pay awful high. Me to be getting five hundred for such a simple little thing as that. You're trating me most royal indade! It's away beyond all I'd be expecting. Sivinteen cints would be a big price for that job. It must be looked into thorough. Just you wait here until I do a minute's turn in the swamp, and then I'll be eschorting you out of the clearing and giving you the answer."

Freckles lifted the overhanging bushes and hurried to the case. He unslung the specimen-box and laid it inside with his hatchet and revolver. He slipped the key in his pocket and went back to Wessner.

"Now for the answer," he said. "Stand up!"

There was iron in his voice, and he was commanding as an outraged general. "Anything you want to be taking off?" he questioned.

Wessner looked the astonishment he felt. "Why, no, Freckles," he said.

"Have the goodness to be calling me Mister McLean," snapped Freckles. "I'm after resarvin' me pet name for the use of me friends! You may stand with your back to the light or be taking any advantage you want."

"Why, what do you mean?" spluttered Wessner.

"I'm manin'," said Freckles tersely, "to lick a quarter-section of hell out of you, and may the Holy Vargin stay me before I leave you here carrion, for your carcass would turn the stummicks of me chickens!"

At the camp that morning, Wessner's conduct had been so palpable an excuse to force a discharge that Duncan moved near McLean and whispered, "Think of the boy, sir?"

McLean was so troubled that, an hour later, he mounted

Nellie and followed Wessner to his home in Wildcat Hollow, only to find that he had left there shortly before, heading for the Limberlost. McLean rode at top speed. When Mrs. Duncan told him that a man answering Wessner's description had gone down the west side of the swamp close noon, he left the mare in her charge and followed on foot. When he heard voices he entered the swamp and silently crept close just in time to hear Wessner whine: "But I can't fight you, Freckles. I hain't done nothing to you. I'm away bigger than you, and you've only one hand."

The Boss slid off his coat and crouched among the bushes, ready to spring; but as Freckles' voice reached him he held himself, with a strong effort, to learn what mettle was in the boy.

"Don't you be wasting of me good time in the numbering of me hands," cried Freckles. "The stringth of me cause will make up for the weakness of me mimbers, and the size of a cowardly thief doesn't count. You'll think all the wild-cats of the Limberlost are turned loose on you whin I come against you, and as for me cause—— I slept with you, Wessner, the night I came down the corduroy like a dirty, friendless tramp, and the Boss was for taking me up, washing, clothing, and feeding me, and giving me a home full of love and tinderness, and a master to look to, and good, well-earned money in the bank. He's trusting me his heartful, and here comes you, you spotted toad of the big road, and insults me, as is an honest Irish gintleman, by hinting that you concaive I'd be willing to shut me eyes and hold fast while you rob him of the thing I was set and paid to guard, and then act the sneak and liar to him, and ruin and eternally blacken the soul of me. You damned rascal," raved Freckles, "be fighting before I forget the laws of a gintlemin's game and split your dirty head with me stick!"

Wessner backed away, mumbling, "But I don't want to hurt you, Freckles!"

"Oh, don't you!" raged the boy, now fairly frothing. "Well, you ain't resembling me none, for I'm itching like death to git me fingers in the face of you."

He danced up, and as Wessner lunged in self-defense, ducked under his arm as a bantam and punched him in the pit of the stomach so that he doubled with a groan. Before Wessner could straighten himself, Freckles was on him, fighting like the wildest fury that ever left the beautiful island. The Dutchman dealt thundering blows that sometimes landed and sent Freckles reeling, and sometimes missed, while he went plunging into the swale with the impetus of them. Freckles could not strike with half Wessner's force, but he could land three blows to the Dutchman's one. It was here that the boy's days of alert watching on the line, the perpetual swinging of the heavy cudgel, and the endurance of all weather stood him in good stead; for he was tough, and agile. He skipped, ducked, and dodged. For the first five minutes he endured fearful punishment. Then Wessner's breath commenced to whistle between his teeth, when Freckles only had begun fighting. He sprang back with shrill laughter.

"Begolly! and will your honour be whistling the hornpipe for me to be dancing of?" he cried.

Spang! went his fist into Wessner's face, and he was past him into the swale.

"And would you be pleased to tune up a little livelier?" he gasped, and clipped his ear as he sprang back. Wessner lunged at him in blind fury. Freckles, seeing an opening, forgot the laws of a gentleman's game and drove the toe of his heavy wading-boot in Wessner's middle until he doubled and fell heavily. In a flash Freckles was on him. For a time McLean could not see what was happening. "Go! Go to him now!" he commanded himself, but so intense was his desire to see the boy win alone that he did not stir.

At last Freckles sprang up and backed away. "Time!" he yelled as a fury. "Be getting up, Mr. Wessner, and don't be afraid of hurting me. I'll let you throw in an extra hand and lick you to me complate satisfaction all the same. Did you hear me call the limit? Will you get up and be facing me?"

As Wessner struggled to his feet, he resembled a battlefield, for his clothing was in ribbons and his face and hands streaming blood.

"I—I guess I got enough," he mumbled.

"Oh, you do?" roared Freckles. "Well this ain't your say. You come on to me ground, lying about me Boss and intimatin' I'd stale from his very pockets. Now will you be standing up and taking your medicine like a man, or getting it poured down the throat of you like a baby? I ain't got enough! This is only just the beginning with me. Be looking out there!"

He sprang against Wessner and sent him rolling. He

attacked the unresisting figure and fought him until he lay limp and quiet and Freckles had no strength left to lift an arm. Then he arose and stepped back, gasping for breath. With his first lungful of air he shouted: "Time!" But the figure of Wessner lay motionless.

Freckles watched him with regardful eye and saw at last that he was completely exhausted. He bent over him, and catching him by the back of the neck, jerked him to his knees. Wessner lifted the face of a whipped cur, and fearing further punishment, burst into shivering sobs, while the tears washed tiny rivulets through the blood and muck. Freckles stepped back, glaring at Wessner, but suddenly the scowl of anger and the ugly disfiguring red faded from the boy's face. He dabbed at a cut on his temple from which issued a tiny crimson stream, and jauntily shook back his hair. His face took on the innocent look of a cherub, and his voice rivalled that of a brooding dove, but into his eyes crept a look of diabolical mischief.

He glanced vaguely around him until he saw his club, seized and twirled it as a drum-major, stuck it upright in the muck, and marched on tiptoe to Wessner, mechanically, as a puppet worked by a string. Bending over, Freckles reached an arm around Wessner's waist and helped him to his feet.

"Careful, now," he cautioned; "be careful, Freddy; there's danger of you hurting me."

Drawing a handkerchief from a back pocket, Freckles tenderly wiped Wessner's eyes and nose.

"Come, Freddy, me child," he admonished Wessner;

"it's time little boys were going home. I've me work to do, and can't be entertaining you any more to-day. Come back to-morrow, if you ain't through yet, and we'll repate the perfarmance. Don't be staring at me so wild like! I would eat you, but I can't afford it. Me earnings, being honest, come slow, and I've no money to be squanderin' on the pailful of Dyspeptic's Delight it would be to taking to work you out of my innards!"

Again an awful wrenching seized McLean. Freckles stepped back as Wessner, tottering and reeling, as a thoroughly drunken man, came toward the path, appearing indeed as if wild-cats had attacked him.

The cudgel spun high in air, and catching it with an expertness acquired by long practice on the line, the boy twirled it a second, shook back his thick hair bonnily, and stepping into the trail, followed Wessner. Because Freckles was Irish, it was impossible to do it silently, so presently his clear tenor rang out, though there were bad catches where he was hard pressed for breath:

"It was the Dutch. It was the Dutch.
Do you think it was the Irish hollered help?
Not much!
It was the Dutch. It was the Dutch——"

Wessner turned and mumbled: "What you following me for? What are you going to do with me?"

Freckles called the Limberlost to witness: "How's that for the ingratitude of a beast? And me troubling mesilf to show him off me territory with the honours of war!"

Then he changed his tone completely and added: "Belike it's this, Freddy. You see, the Boss might come riding down this trail any minute, and the little mare's so wheedlesome that if she'd come on to you in your prisint state all of a sudden, she'd stop that short she'd send Mr. McLean out over the ears of her. No disparagement intinded to the sinse of the mare!" he added hastily.

Wessner belched a fearful oath, while Freckles laughed merrily.

"That's a sample of the thanks a generous act's always for getting," he continued. "Here's me neglictin' me work to eschort you out proper, and you saying such awful words. Freddy," he demanded sternly, "do you want me to soap out your mouth? You don't seem to be realizing it, but if you was to buck into Mr. McLean in your prisint state, without me there to explain matters the chance is he'd cut the liver out of you; and I shouldn't think you'd be wanting such a fine gintleman as him to see that it's white!"

Wessner grew ghastly under his grime and broke into a staggering run.

"And now will you be looking at the manners of him?" questioned Freckles plaintively. "Going without even a 'thank you,' right in the face of all the pains I've taken to make it interesting for him!"

Freckles twirled the club and stood as a soldier at "attention" until Wessner left the clearing, but it was the last scene of that performance. When the boy turned, there was deathly illness on his face, while his legs wavered beneath his weight. He staggered to the case, and opening it he took out a piece of cloth. He dipped it into the water, and sitting on a bench, he wiped the blood and grime from his face, while his breath sucked between his clenched teeth. He was shivering with pain and excitement in spite of himself. He unbuttoned the band of his right sleeve, and turning it back, exposed the blue-lined, calloused whiteness of his maimed arm, now vividly streaked with contusions, while in a series of circular dots the blood oozed slowly. Here Wessner had succeeded in setting his teeth. When Freckles saw what it was he forgave himself the kick in the pit of Wessner's stomach, and cursed fervently and deep.

"Freckles, Freckles," said McLean's voice.

Freckles snatched down his sleeve and arose to his feet.

"Excuse me, sir," he said. "You'll surely be belavin' I thought meself alone."

McLean pushed him carefully to the seat, and bending over him, opened a pocket-case that he carried as regularly as his revolver and watch, for cuts and bruises were of daily occurrence among the gang.

Taking the hurt arm, he turned back the sleeve and bathed and bound the wounds. He examined Freckles' head and body and convinced himself that there was no permanent injury, although the cruelty of the punishment the boy had borne set the Boss shuddering. Then he closed the case, shoved it into his pocket, and sat beside Freckles. All the indescribable beauty of the place was strong around him, but he saw only the bruised face of the suffering boy, who had hedged for the information he wanted as a diplomat, argued as a judge, fought as a sheik, and triumphed as a devil.

When the pain lessened and breath relieved Freckles' pounding heart, he watched the Boss covertly. How had McLean gotten there and how long had he been there? Freckles did not dare ask. At last he arose, and going to the case, took out his revolver and the wire-mending apparatus and locked the door. Then he turned to McLean.

"Have you any orders, sir?" he asked.

"Yes," said McLean, "I have, and you are to follow them to the letter. Turn over that apparatus to me and go straight home. Soak yourself in the hottest bath your skin will bear and go to bed at once. Now hurry."

"Mr. McLean," said Freckles, "it's sorry I am to be telling you, but the afternoon's walking of the line ain't done. You see, I was just for getting to me feet to start, and I was on time, when up came a gintleman, and we got into a little heated argument. It's either settled, or it's just begun, but between us, I'm that late I haven't started for the afternoon yet. I must be going at once, for there's a tree I must find before the day's over."

"You plucky little idiot," growled McLean. "You can't walk the line! I doubt if you can reach Duncan's. Don't you know when you are done up? You go to bed; I'll finish your work."

"Niver!" protested Freckles. "I was just a little done up for the prisint, a minute ago. I'm all right now. Riding-boots are far too low. The day's hot and the walk a good seven miles, sir. Niver!"

As he reached for the outfit he pitched forward and his eyes closed. McLean stretched him on the moss and applied restoratives. When Freckles returned to consciousness, McLean ran to the cabin to tell Mrs. Duncan to have a hot bath ready, and to bring Nellie. That worthy woman promptly filled the wash-boiler, starting a roaring fire under it. She pushed the horse-trough from its base and rolled it to the kitchen.

By the time McLean came again, leading Nellie and holding Freckles on her back, Mrs. Duncan was ready for business. She and the Boss laid Freckles in the trough and poured on hot water until he squirmed. They soaked and massaged him. Then they drew off the hot water and closed his pores with cold. Lastly they stretched him on the floor and chafed, rubbed, and kneaded him until he cried out for mercy. As they rolled him into bed, his eyes dropped shut, but a little later they flared open.

"Mr. McLean," he cried, "the tree! Oh, do be looking after the tree!"

McLean bent over him. "Which tree, Freckles?"

"I don't know exact, sir; but it's on the east line, and the wire is fastened to it. He bragged that you nailed it yourself, sir. You'll know it by the bark having been laid open to the grain somewhere low down. Five hundred dollars he offered me—to be—selling you out—sir!"

Freckles' head rolled over and his eyes dropped shut. McLean towered above the lad. His bright hair waved on the pillow. His face was swollen, and purple with bruises. His left arm, with the hand battered almost out of shape, stretched beside him, and the right, with no hand at all, lay across a chest that was a mass of purple welts. McLean's mind travelled to the night, almost a year before, when he had engaged Freckles, a stranger.

The Boss bent, covering the hurt arm with one hand and laying the other with a caress on the boy's forehead. Freckles stirred at his touch, and whispered as softly as the swallows under the eaves: "If you're coming this way —to-morrow—be pleased to step over—and we'll repate—the chorus softly!"

"Bless the gritty devil," muttered McLean.

Then he went out and told Mrs. Duncan to keep close watch on Freckles, also to send Duncan to him at the swamp the minute he came home. Following the trail to the line and back to the scene of the fight, the Boss entered Freckles' study quietly, as if his spirit, sleeping there, might be roused, and gazed around with astonished eyes.

How had the boy conceived it? What a picture he had wrought in living colours! He had the heart of a painter. He had the soul of a poet. The Boss stepped carefully over the velvet carpet to touch the walls of crisp verdure with gentle fingers. He stood long beside the flower-bed, and gazed at the banked wall of bright bloom as if he doubted its reality.

Where had Freckles ever found, and how had he transplanted such ferns? As McLean turned from them he stopped suddenly.

He had reached the door of the cathedral. That which Freckles had attempted would have been patent to any one. What had been in the heart of the shy, silent boy when he had found that long, dim stretch of forest, decorated its entrance, cleared and smoothed its aisle, and carpeted its altar? What veriest work of God was in these mighty living pillars and the arched dome of green! How similar to stained cathedral windows were the long openings between the trees, filled with rifts of blue, rays of gold, and the shifting emerald of leaves! Where could be found mosaics to match this aisle paved with living colour and glowing lights? Was Freckles a devout Christian, and did he worship here? Or was he an untaught heathen, and down this vista of entrancing loveliness did Pan come piping, and dryads, nymphs, and fairies dance for him?

Who can fathom the heart of a boy? McLean had been thinking of Freckles as a creature of unswerving honesty, courage, and faithfulness. Here was evidence of a heart aching for beauty, art, companionship, worship. It was writ large all over the floor, walls, and furnishing of that little Limberlost clearing.

When Duncan came, McLean told him the story of the fight, and they laughed until they cried. Then they started around the line in search of the tree.

Said Duncan: "Now the boy is in for sore trouble!"

"I hope not," answered McLean. "You never in all your life saw a cur whipped so completely. He won't come back for the repetition of the chorus. We surely can find the tree. If we can't, Freckles can. I will bring enough of the gang to take it out at once. That will insure peace for a time, at least, and I am hoping that in a month more the whole gang may be moved here. It soon will be fall, and then, if he will go, I intend to send Freckles to my mother to be educated. With his quickness of mind and body and a few years' good help he can do anything. Why, Duncan, I'd give a hundred-dollar bill if you could have been here and seen for yourself."

"Yes, and I'd 'a' done murder," muttered the big teamster. "I hope, sir, ye will make good your plans for Freckles, though I'd as soon see ony born child o' my ain taken from our home. We love the lad, me and Sarah."

Locating the tree was easy, because it was so well identified. When the rumble of the big lumber-wagons passing the cabin on the way to the swamp wakened Freckles next morning, he sprang up and was soon following them. He was so sore and stiff that every movement was torture at first, but he grew easier, and shortly did not suffer so much. McLean scolded him for coming, yet in his heart triumphed over every new evidence of fineness in the boy.

The tree was a giant maple, and so precious that they almost dug it out by the roots. When it was down, cut in lengths, and loaded, there was yet an empty wagon. As they were gathering up their tools to go, Duncan said: "There's a big hollow tree somewhere mighty close here that I've been wanting for a watering-trough for my stock; the one I have is so small. The Portland company cut this for elm butts last year, and it's six feet diameter and hollow for forty feet. It was a buster! While the men are here and there is an empty wagon, why mightn't I load it on and tak' it up to the barn as we pass?"

McLean said he was very willing, ordered the driver to break line and load the log, detailing men to assist. He told Freckles to ride on a section of the maple with him, but now the boy asked to enter the swamp with Duncan.

"I don't see why you want to go," said McLean. "I have no business to let you out to-day at all."

"It's me chickens," whispered Freckles in distress.

"You see, I was just after finding yesterday, from me new book, how they do be nesting in hollow trees, and there ain't any too many in the swamp. There's just a chance that they might be in that one."

"Go ahead," said McLean. "That's a different story. If they happen to be there, why tell Duncan he must give up the tree until they have finished with it."

Then he climbed on a wagon and was driven away. Freckles hurried into the swamp. He was a little behind, yet he could see the men. Before he overtook them, they had turned from the west road and had entered the swamp toward the east.

They stopped at the trunk of a monstrous prostrate log. It had been cut three feet from the ground, over three-fourths of the way through, and had fallen toward the east, the body of the log still resting on the stump. The underbrush was almost impenetrable, but Duncan plunged in and with a crowbar began tapping along the trunk to decide how far it was hollow, so that they would know where to cut. As they waited his decision, there came from the mouth of it—on wings—a large black bird that swept over their heads.

Freckles danced wildly. "It's me chickens! Oh, it's me chickens!" he shouted. "Oh, Duncan, come quick! You've found the nest of me precious chickens!"

Duncan hurried to the mouth of the log, but Freckles was before him. He crashed through poison-vines and underbrush regardless of any danger, and climbed on the stump. When Duncan came he was shouting like a wild man.

"It's hatched!" he yelled. "Oh, me big chicken has hatched out me little chicken, and there's another egg. I can see it plain, and oh, the funny little white baby! Oh, Duncan, can you see me little white chicken?"

Duncan could easily see it; so could every one else. Freckles crept into the log and tenderly carried the hissing, blinking little bird to the light in a leaf-lined hat. The men found it sufficiently wonderful to satisfy even Freckles, who had forgotten he was ever sore or stiff, and coddled over it with every blarneying term of endearment he knew.

Duncan gathered his tools. "Deal's off, boys!" he said cheerfully. "This log mauna be touched until Freckles' chaukies have finished with it. We might as weel gang. Better put it back, Freckles. It's just out, and it may chill. Ye will probably hae twa the morn."

Freckles crept into the log and carefully deposited the baby beside the egg. When he came back, he said: "I made a big mistake not to be bringing the egg out with the baby, but I was fearing to touch it. It's shaped like a hen's egg, and it's big as a turkey's, and the beautifulest blue—just splattered with big brown splotches, like me book said, precise. Bet you never saw such a sight as it made on the yellow of the rotten wood beside that funny leathery-faced little white baby."

"Tell you what, Freckles," said one of the teamsters: "Have you ever heard of this Bird Woman who goes all over the country with a camera and makes pictures? She made some on my brother Jim's place last summer, and Jim's so wild about them he quits ploughing and goes after her about every nest he finds. He helps her all he can to take them, and then she gives him a picture. Jim's so proud of what he has he keeps them in the Bible. He shows them to everybody that comes, and brags about how he helped. If you're smart, you'll send for her and she'll come and make a picture just like life. If you help her, she will give you one. It would be uncommon pretty to keep, after your birds are gone. I dunno what they are. I never see their like before. They must be something rare. Any you fellows ever see a bird like that hereabouts?"

No one ever had.

"Well," said the teamster, "failing to get this log lets me off till noon, and I'm going to town. I go right past her place. I've a big notion to stop and tell her. If she drives straight back in the swamp on the west road, and turns east at this big sycamore, she can't miss finding the tree, even if Freckles ain't here to show her. Jim says her work is a credit to the State she lives in, and any man is a measly creature who isn't willing to help her all he can. My old daddy used to say that all there was to religion was doing to the other fellow what you'd want him to do to you, and if I was making a living taking bird pictures, seems to me I'd be mighty glad for a chance to take one like that. So I'll just stop and tell her, and by gummy! maybe she will give me a picture of the little white sucker for my trouble."

Freckles touched his arm.

"Will she be rough with it?" he asked.

"Government land! No!" said the teamster. "She's dead down on anybody that shoots a bird or tears up a nest. Why, she's half killing herself in all kinds of places and weather to teach people to love and protect the birds. She's that plum careful of them that Jim's wife says she has Jim a standin' like a big fool holding an ombrelly over them when they are young and tender until she gets a focus, whatever that is. Jim says there ain't a bird on his place that don't actually seem to like having her around after she has wheedled them a few days, and the pictures she takes nobody would ever believe who didn't stand by and see."

"Will you be sure to tell her to come?" asked Freckles.

Duncan slept at home that night. He heard Freckles slipping out early the next morning, but he was too sleepy to wonder why, until he came to do his morning chores. When he found that none of his stock was at all thirsty, and saw the water-trough brimming, he knew that the boy was trying to make up to him for the loss of the big trough that he had been so anxious to have.

"Bless his fool little hot heart!" said Duncan. "And him so sore it is tearing him to move for anything. Nae wonder he has us all loving him!"

Freckles was moving briskly, and his heart was so happy that he forgot all about the bruises. He hurried around the trail, and on his way down the east side he went to see the chickens. The mother-bird was on the nest. He was afraid the other egg might be hatching, so he did not venture to disturb her. He made the round and reached his study early. He ate his lunch, but did not need to start on the second trip until the middle of the afternoon. He would have long hours to work on his flower-bed, improve his study, and learn about his chickens. Lovingly he set his room in order and watered the flowers and carpet. He had chosen for his resting-place the coolest spot on the west side, where there was almost always a breeze; but to-day the heat was so intense that it penetrated even there.

"I'm mighty glad there's nothing calling me inside!" he said. "There's no bit of air stirring, and it will just be steaming. Oh, but it's luck Duncan found the nest before it got so unbearing hot! I might have missed it altogether. Wouldn't it have been a shame to lose that sight? The cunning little divil! When he gets to toddling down that log to meet me, won't he be a circus? Wonder if he'll be as graceful a performer afoot as his father and mother?"

The heat became more insistent. Noon came; Freckles ate his dinner and settled for an hour or two on a bench with a book.

CHAPTER V

Wherein an Angel Materializes and a Man Worships

CHAPTER V

Wherein an Angel Materializes and a Man Worships

PERHAPS there was a breath of sound—Freckles never afterward could remember—but for some reason he lifted his head as the bushes parted and the face of an angel looked between. Saints, nymphs, and fairies had floated down his cathedral aisle for him many times, with forms and voices of exquisite beauty.

Parting the wild roses at the entrance was beauty of which Freckles never had dreamed. Was it real or would it vanish as the other dreams? He dropped his book, and rising to his feet, went a step closer, gazing intently. This was real flesh and blood. It was in every way kin to the Limberlost, for no bird of its branches swung with easier grace than this dainty young thing rocked on the bit of morass on which she stood. A sapling beside her was not straighter or rounder than her slender form. Her soft, waving hair clung around her face from the heat, and curled over her shoulders. It was all of one piece with the gold of the sun that filtered between the branches. Her eyes were the deepest blue of the iris, her lips the reddest red of the foxfire, while her cheeks were exactly of the same satin as the wild rose petals caressing them. She was smiling at

Freckles in perfect confidence, and she cried: "Oh, I'm so delighted that I've found you!"

The wildly leaping heart of Freckles burst from his body and fell in the black swamp-muck at her feet with such a thud that he did not understand how she could avoid hearing. He really felt that if she looked down she would see.

Incredulous, he quavered: "An'—an' was you looking for me?"

"I hoped I might find you," said the Angel. "You see, I didn't do as I was told, and I'm lost. The Bird Woman said I should wait in the carriage until she came back. She's been gone hours. It's a perfect Turkish bath in there, and I'm all lumpy with mosquito bites. Just when I thought that I couldn't bear it another minute, along came the biggest Papilio Ajax you ever saw. I knew how pleased she'd be, so I ran after it. It flew so slow and so low that I thought a dozen times I had it. Then all at once it went from sight above the trees, and I couldn't find my way back to save me. I think I've walked more than an hour. I have been mired to my knees. A thorn raked my arm until it is bleeding, and I'm so tired and warm."

She parted the bushes farther. Freckles saw that her blue cotton frock clung to her, limp with perspiration. It was torn across the breast. One sleeve hung open from shoulder to elbow. A thorn had torn her arm until it was covered with blood, and the gnats and mosquitoes were clustering around it. Her feet were in lace hose and low shoes. Freckles gasped. In the Limberlost in low shoes! He caught an armful of moss from his carpet and buried it in the ooze in front of her for a footing.

"Come out here so I can see where you are stepping. Quick, for the life of you!" he ordered.

She smiled on him indulgently.

"Why?" she inquired.

"Did anybody let you come here and not be telling you of the snakes?" urged Freckles.

"We met Mr. McLean on the corduroy, and he did say something about snakes, I believe. The Bird Woman put on leather leggings, and a nice, parboiled time she must be having! Worse dose I ever endured, and I'd nothing to do but swelter."

"Will you be coming out of there?" groaned Freckles.

She laughed as if it were a fine joke.

"Maybe if I'd be telling you I killed a rattler curled upon that same place you're standing, as long as me body and the thickness of me arm, you'd be moving where I can see your footing," he urged insistently.

"What a perfectly delightful little brogue you speak," she said. "My father is Irish, and half should be enough to entitle me to that much. 'Maybe—if I'd—be telling you,'" she imitated, rounding and accenting each word carefully.

Freckles was beginning to feel a wildness in his head. He had derided Wessner at that same hour yesterday. Now his own eyes were filling with tears.

"If you were understanding the danger!" he continued desperately.

"Oh, I don't think there is much!"

She tilted on the morass.

"If you killed one snake here, it's probably all there is near; and anyway, the Bird Woman says a rattlesnake is a gentleman and always gives warning before he strikes. I don't hear any rattling. Do you?"

"Would you be knowing it if you did?" asked Freckles, almost impatiently.

How the laugh of the young thing rippled!

"'Would I be knowing it?'" she mocked. "You should see the swamps of Michigan where they dump rattlers from the marl-dredgers three and four at a time!"

Freckles stood astounded. She did know. She was not in the least afraid. She was depending on a rattlesnake to live up to his share of the contract and rattle in time for her to move. The one characteristic an Irishman admires in a woman, above all others, is courage. Freckles worshipped anew. He changed his tactics.

"I'd be pleased to be receiving you at me front door," he said, "but as you have arrived at the back, will you come in and be seated?"

He waved toward a bench. The Angel came instantly.

"Oh, how lovely and cool!" she cried.

As she moved across his room, Freckles had difficult work to keep from falling on his knees; for they were very weak, while he was hard driven by an impulse to worship.

"Did you arrange this?" she asked.

"Yis," said Freckles simply.

"Some one must come with a big canvas and copy each side of it," she said. "I never saw anything so beautiful! How I wish I might remain here with you! I will, some day, if you will let me; but now, if you can spare the time, will you help me find the carriage? If the Bird Woman comes back and I am gone, she will be almost distracted."

"Did you come on the west road?" asked Freckles.

"I think so," she said. "The man who told the Bird Woman said that was the only place the wires were down. We drove away in, and it was dreadful—over stumps and logs, and we mired to the hubs. I suppose you know, though. I should have stayed in the carriage, but I was so tired. I never dreamed of getting lost. I suspect I will be scolded finely. I go with the Bird Woman half the time during the summer vacations. My father says I learn a lot more than I do at school, and get it straight. I never came within a smell of being lost before. I thought, at first, it was going to be horrid; but since I've found you, maybe it will be good fun after all."

Freckles was amazed to hear himself excusing: "It was so hot in there. You couldn't be expected to bear it for hours and not be moving. I can take you around the trail almost to where you were. Then you can sit in the carriage, and I will go find the Bird Woman."

"You'll be killed if you do! When she stays this long, it means that she has a focus on something. You see, when she has a focus, and lies in the weeds and water for hours, and the sun bakes her, and things crawl over her, and then some one comes along and scares her bird away just as she has it coaxed up—why, she *kills* them. If I melt, you won't go after her. She's probably blistered and half eaten up; but she never will quit until she is satisfied."

"Then it will be safer to be taking care of you," suggested Freckles.

"Now you're talking sense!" said the Angel.

"May I try to help your arm?" he asked.

"Have you any idea how it hurts?" she parried.

"A little," said Freckles.

"Well, Mr. McLean said we'd probably find his son here——"

"His son!" cried Freckles.

"That's what he said. And that you would do anything you could for us; and that we could trust you with our lives. But I would have trusted you anyway, if I hadn't known a thing about you. Say, your father is rampaging proud of you, isn't he?"

"I don't know," answered the dazed Freckles.

"Well, call on me if you want reliable information. He's so proud of you he is all swelled up like the toad in Æsop's Fables. If you have ever had an arm hurt like this, and can do anything, why, for pity sake, do it!"

She turned back her sleeve, holding toward Freckles an arm of palest cameo, shaped so exquisitely that no sculptor could have chiselled it.

Freckles unlocked his case, and taking out some cotton cloth, he tore it in strips. Then he brought a bucket of the cleanest water he could find. She yielded herself to his touch as a baby, and he bathed away the blood and bandaged the ugly, ragged wound. He finished his surgery by lapping the torn sleeve over the cloth and binding it down with a piece of twine, with the Angel's help about the knots.

Freckles worked with trembling fingers and a face tense with earnestness.

"Is it feeling any better?" he asked.

"Oh, it's well now!" cried the Angel. "It doesn't hurt at all, any more."

"I'm mighty glad," said Freckles. "But you had best go and be having your doctor fix it right, the minute you get home."

"Oh, bother! A little scratch like that!" jeered the Angel. "My blood is perfectly pure. It will heal in three days."

"It's cut cruel deep. It might be making a scar," faltered Freckles, his eyes on the ground. "'Twould—'twould be an awful pity. A doctor might know something to prevent it."

"Why, I never thought of that!" exclaimed the Angel.

"I noticed you didn't," said Freckles softly. "I don't know much about it, but it seems as if most girls would."

The Angel thought intently, while Freckles still knelt beside her. Suddenly she gave herself an impatient little shake, lifted her glorious eyes full to his, and the smile that swept her sweet, young face was the loveliest thing that Freckles ever had seen.

"Don't let's bother about it," she proposed, with the faintest hint of a confiding gesture toward him. "It won't make a scar. Why, it couldn't, when you have dressed it so nicely."

The velvety touch of her warm arm was tingling in Freckles' finger-tips. Dainty laces and fine white puffs peeped through her torn dress. There were beautiful rings on her fingers. Every article she wore was of the finest material and in excellent taste. There was the trembling Limberlost guard in his coarse clothing, with his cotton-rags and his old pail of swamp-water. Freckles was sufficiently accustomed to contrasts to notice them, and sufficiently fine to be hurt by them always.

He lifted his eyes with a shadowy pain in them to hers, and found them of serene, unconscious purity. What she had said was straight from a kind, untainted, young heart. She meant every word of it. Freckles' soul sickened. He scarcely knew whether he could muster strength to stand.

"We must go and hunt for the carriage," said the Angel, rising.

In instant alarm for her, Freckles sprang up, grasped the cudgel, and led the way, sharply watching every step. He went as close the log as he felt that he dared, and with a little searching found the carriage. He cleared a path for the Angel, and with a sigh of relief saw her enter it safely. The heat was intense. She pushed the damp hair from her temples.

"This is a shame!" said Freckles. "You'll never be coming here again."

"Oh yes I shall!" said the Angel. "The Bird Woman says that these birds remain over a month in the nest and she would like to make a picture every few days for seven or eight weeks, perhaps."

Freckles barely escaped crying aloud for joy.

"Then don't you ever be torturing yourself and your horse to be coming in here again," he said. "I'll show you a way to drive almost to the nest on the east trail, and then you can come around to my room and stay while the Bird Woman works. It's nearly always cool there, and there's comfortable seats, and water."

"Oh! did you have drinking-water there?" she cried. "I was never so thirsty or so hungry in my life, but I thought I wouldn't mention it."

"And I had not the wit to be seeing!" wailed Freckles. "I can be getting you a good drink in no time."

He turned to the trail.

"Please wait a minute," called the Angel. "What's your name? I want to think about you while you are gone."

Freckles lifted his face with the brown rift across it and smiled quizzically.

"Freckles?" she guessed, with a peal of laughter. "And mine is——"

"I'm knowing yours," interrupted Freckles.

"I don't believe you do. What is it?" asked the girl.

"You won't be getting angry?"

"Not until I've had the water, at least."

It was Freckles' turn to laugh. He whipped off his big, floppy straw-hat, stood uncovered before her, and said, in the sweetest of all the sweet tones of his voice: "There's nothing you could be but the Swamp Angel."

The girl laughed happily.

Once out of her sight, Freckles ran every step of the way to the cabin. Mrs. Duncan gave him a small bucket of water, cool from the well. He carried it in the crook of his right arm, and a basket filled with bread and butter, cold meat, apple pie, and pickles, in his left hand.

"Pickles are kind o' cooling," said Mrs. Duncan.

Then Freckles ran again.

The Angel was on her knees, reaching for the bucket, as he came up.

"Be drinking slow," he cautioned her.

"Oh!" she cried, with a long breath of satisfaction. "It's so good! You are more than kind to bring it!"

Freckles stood blinking in the dazzling glory of her smile until he scarcely could see to lift the basket.

"Mercy!" she exclaimed. "I think I had better be naming you the 'Angel.' My Guardian Angel."

"Yis," said Freckles. "I look the character every day —but to-day most emphatic!"

"Angels don't go by looks," laughed the girl. "Your father told us you had been scrapping. But he told us why. I'd gladly wear all your cuts and bruises if I could do anything that would make my father look as peacocky as yours did. He strutted about proper I never saw any one look prouder."

"Did he say he was proud of me?" marvelled Freckles.

"He didn't need to," answered the Angel. "He was radiating pride from every pore. Now, have you brought me your dinner?"

"I had my dinner two hours ago," answered Freckles.

"Honest Injun?" bantered the Angel.

"Honest! I brought that on purpose for you."

"Well, if you knew how hungry I am, you would know how thankful I am, to the dot," said the Angel.

"Then you be eating," cried the happy Freckles.

The Angel sat on a big camera, spread the lunch on the carriage-seat, and divided it in halves. The daintiest parts she could select she carefully put back into the basket. The remainder she ate. Again Freckles found her of the swamp, for though she was almost ravenous, she managed her food as gracefully as his little yellow fellow, and her every movement was easy and charming. As he watched her with famished eyes, Freckles told her of his birds, flowers, and books, and never realized what he was doing.

He led the horse to a deep pool that he knew of, and the tortured creature drank greedily, and lovingly rubbed him with its nose as he wiped down its welted body with grass. Suddenly the Angel cried: "There comes the Bird Woman!"

Freckles had intended leaving before she came, but now he was glad indeed to be there, for a warmer, more worn, and worse bitten creature he never had seen. She was staggering under a load of cameras and paraphernalia. Freckles ran to her aid. He took all he could carry of her load, stowed it in the back of the carriage, and helped her in. The Angel gave her water, knelt and unfastened the leggings, bathed her face, and offered the lunch.

Freckles brought the horse. He was not sure about the harness, but the Angel knew, and soon they left the swamp. Then he showed them how to reach the chicken tree from the outside, indicated a cooler place for the horse, and told them how, the next time they came, the Angel could find his room while she waited.

The Bird Woman finished her lunch, and lay back, almost too tired to speak.

"Were you for getting Little Chicken's picture?" Freckles asked.

"Finely!" she answered. "He posed splendidly. But

I couldn't do anything with his mother. She will require coaxing."

"The Lord be praised!" muttered Freckles under his breath.

The Bird Woman began to feel better.

"Why do you call the baby vulture 'Little Chicken'?" she asked, leaning toward Freckles in an interested manner.

"'Twas Duncan began it," said Freckles. "You see, through the fierce cold of winter the birds of the swamp were almost starving. It is mighty lonely here, and they were all the company I was having. I got to carrying scraps and grain down to them. Duncan was that ginerous he was giving me of his wheat and corn from his chickens' feed, and he called the birds me swamp chickens. Then when these big black fellows came, Mr. McLean said they were our nearest kind to some in the old world that they called 'Pharaoh's Chickens,' and he called mine 'Freckles' Chickens.'"

"Good enough!" cried the Bird Woman, her splotched purple face lighting with interest. "You must shoot something for them occasionally, and I'll bring more food when I come. If you will help me keep them until I get my series, I'll give you a copy of each study I make, mounted in a book."

Freckles drew a deep breath.

"I'll be doing me very best," he promised, and from the deeps he meant it.

"I wonder if that other egg is going to hatch?" mused the Bird Woman. "I am afraid not. It should have pipped to-day. Isn't it a beauty! I never before saw either an egg or the young. They are rare this far north."

"So Mr. McLean said," answered Freckles.

Before they drove away, the Bird Woman thanked him for his kindness to the Angel and to her. She gave him her hand at parting, and Freckles joyfully realized that this was going to be another person for him to love. He could not remember, after they had driven away, that they even had noticed his missing hand, and for the first time in his life he had forgotten it.

When the Bird Woman and the Angel were on the home road, she told of the little corner of paradise into which she had strayed and of her new name. The Bird Woman looked at the girl and guessed its appropriateness.

"Did you know Mr. McLean had a son?" asked the Angel. "Isn't the little accent he has, and the way he twists a sentence, too dear? And isn't it too old-fashioned and funny to hear him call his father 'mister'?"

"It sounds too good to be true," said the Bird Woman, answering the last question first. "I am so tired of these present-day young men who patronizingly call their fathers 'Dad,' 'Governor,' 'Old Man,' and 'Old Chap,' that the boy's attitude of respect and deference appealed to me as being fine as silk. There must be something rare about that young man."

She did not find it necessary to tell the Angel that for several years she had known the man who so proudly proclaimed himself Freckles' father to be a bachelor and a

Scotchman. The Bird Woman had a fine way of attending strictly to her own business.

Freckles turned to the trail, but he stopped at every wild brier to study the pink satin of the petals. She was not of his world, and better than any other he knew it; but she might be his Angel, and he was dreaming of naught but blind, silent worship. He finished the happiest day of his life, and that night he returned to the swamp as if drawn by invisible force. That Wessner would try for his revenge, he knew. That he would be abetted by Black Jack was almost certain, but fear had fled the happy heart of Freckles. He had kept his trust. He had won the respect of the Boss. No one ever could wipe from his heart the flood of holy adoration that had welled with the coming of his Angel. He would do his best, and trust for strength to meet the dark day of reckoning that he knew would come sooner or later. He swung round the trail, briskly tapping the wire, and singing in a voice that scarcely could have been surpassed for sweetness.

At the edge of the clearing he came into the bright moonlight, and there sat McLean on his mare. Freckles hurried to him.

"Is there trouble?" he inquired anxiously.

"That's what I wanted to ask you," said the Boss. "I stopped at the cabin to see you a minute, before I turned in, and they said you had come down here. You must not do it, Freckles. The swamp is none too healthful at any time, and at night it is rank poison."

Freckles stood combing his fingers through Nellie's

mane, while the dainty creature was twisting her head for his caresses. He pushed back his hat and looked into McLean's face. "It's come to the 'sleep with one eye open,' sir. I'm not looking for anything to be happening for a week or two, but it's bound to come, and soon. If I'm to keep me trust as I've promised you and meself, I've to live here mostly until the gang comes. You must be knowing that, sir."

"I'm afraid it's true, Freckles," said McLean. "And I've decided to double the guard until we come. It will be only a few weeks, now; and I'm so anxious for you that you must not be left alone further. If anything should happen to you, Freckles, it would spoil one of the very dearest plans of my life."

Freckles heard with dismay the proposition to place a second guard.

"Oh! no, no, Mr. McLean," he cried. "Not for the world! I wouldn't be having a stranger around, scaring me birds and tramping up me study, and disturbing all me ways, for any money! I am all the guard you need! I will be faithful! I will turn over the lease with no tree missing—on me life, I will! Oh, don't be sending another man to set them saying I turned coward and asked for help. It will just kill the honour of me heart if you do it. The only thing I want is another gun. If it railly comes to trouble, six cartridges ain't many, and you know I am slow-like about reloading."

McLean reached into his hip pocket and handed a shining big revolver to Freckles, who slipped it beside the one already in his belt.

Then the Boss sat brooding.

"Freckles," he said at last, "we never know the timber of a man's soul until something cuts into him deeply and brings the grain out strong. You've the making of a mighty fine piece of furniture, my boy, and you shall have your own way these few weeks yet. Then, if you will go, I intend to take you to the city and educate you, and you are to be my son, my lad—my own son!"

Freckles twisted his fingers in Nellie's mane to steady himself.

"But why should you be doing that, sir?" he faltered.

McLean slid his arm around the boy's shoulders and gathered him close.

"Because I love you, Freckles," he said simply.

Freckles lifted a white face. "My God, sir!" he whispered. "Oh, my God!"

McLean tightened his clasp a second longer, then he rode down the trail.

Freckles lifted his hat and faced the sky. The harvest moon looked down, sheeting the swamp in silver glory. The Limberlost sang her night song. The swale softly rustled in the wind. Winged things of night brushed his face; and still Freckles gazed upward, trying to fathom these things that had come to him. There was no help from the sky. It seemed far away, cold, and blue. The earth, where flowers blossomed, angels walked, and love could be found, was better. But to One, above, he must make acknowledgment for these miracles. His lips moved and he began talking softly.

"Thank You for each separate good thing that has come

to me," he said, "and above all for the falling of the feather. For if it didn't really fall from an angel, its falling brought an Angel, and if it's in the great heart of You to exercise Yourself any further about me; oh, do please to be taking good care of her!"

CHAPTER VI

Wherein a Fight Occurs and Women Shoot Straight

CHAPTER VI

Wherein a Fight Occurs and Women Shoot Straight

THE following morning Freckles, inexpressibly happy, circled the Limberlost. He kept snatches of song ringing, as well as the wires. His heart was so full that tears of joy glistened in his eyes. He rigorously strove to divide his thought evenly between McLean and the Angel. He realized to the fullest the debt he already owed the Boss and the magnitude of last night's declaration and promises. He was hourly planning to deliver his trust and then enter with equal zeal on whatever task his beloved Boss saw fit to set him next. He wanted to be ready to meet every device that Wessner and Black Jack could think of to outwit him. He recognized their double leverage, for if they succeeded in felling even one tree McLean became liable for his wager.

Freckles' brow wrinkled in his effort to think deeply and strongly, but from every swaying wild rose the Angel beckoned to him. When he crossed Sleepy Snake Creek and the goldfinch, waiting as ever, challenged: "*See me?*" Freckles saw the dainty swaying grace of the Angel instead. What is a man to do with an Angel who dismembers herself and scatters over a whole swamp, thrusting a vivid reminder upon him at every turn?

Freckles counted the days. This first one he could do little but test his wires, sing broken snatches, and dream; but before the week would bring her again he could do many things. He would carry all his books to the swamp to show to her. He would complete his flower-bed, arrange every detail he had planned for his room, and make of it a bower fairies might envy. He must devise a way to keep water cool. He would ask Mrs. Duncan for a double lunch and an especially nice one the day of her next coming, so that if the Bird Woman happened to be late, the Angel might not suffer from thirst and hunger. He would tell her to bring heavy leather leggings, so that he might take her on a trip around the trail. She should make friends with all of his chickens and see their nests.

On the line he talked of her incessantly.

"You needn't be thinking," he said to the goldfinch, "that because I'm coming down this line alone day after day, it's always to be so. Some of these times you'll be swinging on this wire, and you'll see me coming, and you'll swing, skip, and flirt yourself around, and chip up right spunky: '*See me?*' I'll be saying 'See you? Oh, Lord! See her!' You'll look, and there she'll stand. The sunshine won't look gold any more, or the roses pink, or the sky blue, because she'll be the pinkest, bluest, goldest thing of all. You'll be yelling yourself hoarse with the jealousy of her. The saw-bird will stretch his neck out of joint, and she'll turn the heads of all the flowers. Where-ever she goes, I can go back afterward and see the things she's seen, walk the path she's walked, hear the grasses whispering over all she's said; and if there's a place too swampy for her bits of feet; Holy Mother! maybe—maybe she'd be putting the beautiful arms of her around me neck and letting me carry her over!"

Freckles shivered as with a chill. He sent the cudgel whirling skyward, dexterously caught it, and set it spinning.

"You damned presumptuous fool!" he cried. "The thing for you to be thinking of would be to stretch in the muck for the feet of her to be walking over, and then you could hold yourself holy to be even of that service to her.

"Maybe she'll be wanting the cup me blue-and-brown chickens raised their babies in. Perhaps she'd like to stop at the pool and see me bullfrog that had the goodness to take on human speech to show me the way out of me trouble. If there's any feathers falling that day, why, it's from the wings of me chickens—it's sure to be, for the only Angel outside the gates will be walking this timber-line, and every step of the way I'll be holding me breath and praying that she don't unfold wings and sail away before the hungry eyes of me."

So Freckles dreamed his dreams, made his plans, and watched his line. He counted not only the days, but the hours of each day. As he told them off, every one bringing her closer, he grew happier in the prospect of her coming. He managed daily to leave some offering at the big elm log for his black chickens. He slipped under the line at every passing, and went to make sure that nothing was molesting them. Though it was a long trip, he paid them several extra visits a day for fear a snake, hawk, or fox might have found the baby. For now his chickens not only represented all his former interest in them, but they furnished the inducement that was bringing his Angel.

Possibly he could find other subjects that the Bird Woman wanted. The teamster had said that his brother went after her every time he found a nest. He never had counted the nests that he knew of, and it might be that among all the birds of the swamp some would be rare to her.

The feathered folk of the Limberlost were practically undisturbed save by their natural enemies. It was very probable that among his chickens others as odd as the big black ones could be found. If she wanted pictures of half-grown birds, he could pick up fifty in one morning's trip around the line, for he had fed, handled, and made friends with them ever since their eyes opened.

He had gathered bugs and worms all spring as he noticed them on the grass and bushes, and dropped them into the first little open mouth he had found. The babies gladly had accepted this queer tri-parent addition to their natural providers.

When the week has passed, Freckles had his room crisp and glowing with fresh living things that represented every colour of the swamp. He carried bark and filled all the muckiest places of the trail.

It was middle July. The heat of the past few days had dried the water around and through the Limberlost, so that it was possible to cross it on foot in almost any direction—if one had an idea of direction and did not become completely lost in its rank tangle of vegetation and bushes. The brighter hued flowers were opening. The trumpet-creepers were flaunting their gorgeous horns of red and gold sweetness from the tops of lordly oak and elm, and below entire pools were pink-sheeted in mallow bloom.

The heat was doing one other thing that was bound to make Freckles, as a good Irishman, shiver. As the swale dried, its inhabitants were seeking the cooler depths of the swamp. They liked neither the heat nor leaving the field-mice, moles, and young rabbits of their chosen location. He saw them crossing the trail every day as the heat grew intense. The rattlers were sadly forgetting their manners, for they struck on no provocation whatever, and did not even remember to rattle afterward. Daily Freckles was compelled to drive big black snakes and blue racers from the nests of his chickens. Often the terrified squalls of the parent birds would reach him far down the line and he would run to rescue the babies.

He saw the Angel when the carriage turned from the corduroy into the clearing. They stopped at the west entrance to the swamp, waiting for him to precede them down the trail, as he had told them it was safest for the horse that he should do. They followed the east line to a point opposite the big chickens' tree, and Freckles carried in the cameras and showed the Bird Woman a path he had cleared to the log. He explained to her the effect the heat was having on the snakes, and creeping back to Little Chicken, brought him to the light. As she worked at setting up her camera, he told her of the birds of the line, while she stared at him, wide-eyed and incredulous.

They arranged that Freckles should drive the carriage into the east entrance in the shade and then take the horse toward the north to a better place he knew. Then he was to entertain the Angel at his study or on the line until the Bird Woman finished her work and came to them.

"This will take only a little time," she said. "I know where to set the camera now, and Little Chicken is big enough to be good and too small to run away or to act very ugly, so I will be coming soon to see about those nests. I have ten plates along, and I surely won't use more than two on him; so perhaps I can get some nests or young birds this morning."

Freckles almost flew, for his dream had come true so soon. He was walking the timber-line and the Angel was following him. He asked to be excused for going first, because he wanted to be sure the trail was safe for her. She laughed at his fears, telling him that it was the polite thing for him to do, anyway.

"Oh!" said Freckles, "so you was after knowing that? Well, I didn't s'pose you did, and I was afraid you'd think me wanting in respect to be preceding you!"

The astonished Angel looked at him, caught the irrepressible gleam of Irish fun in his eyes, so they stood and laughed together.

Freckles did not realize how he was talking that morning. He showed her many of the beautiful nests and eggs of the line. She could identify a number of them, but of some she was ignorant, so they made notes of the number and colour of the eggs, material, and construction of nest, colour, size, and shape of the birds, and went to find them in the book.

At his room, when Freckles had lifted the overhanging

bushes and stepped back for her to enter, his heart was all out of time and place. The study was vastly more beautiful than a week previous. The Angel drew a deep breath and stood gazing first at one side, then at another, then far down the cathedral aisle. "It's just fairy-land!" she cried, ecstatically. Then she turned and stared at Freckles as she had at his handiwork.

"What are you planning to be?" she asked wonderingly.

"Whatever Mr. McLean wants me to," he replied.

"What do you do most?" she asked.

"Watch me lines."

"I don't mean work!"

"Oh, in me spare time I keep me room and study in me books."

"Do you work on the room or the books most?"

"On the room only what it takes to keep it up, and the rest of the time on me books."

The Angel studied him closely. "Well, maybe you are going to be a great scholar," she said, "but you don't look it. Your face isn't right for that, but it's got something big in it—something really great. I must find out what it is and then you must work on it. Your father is expecting you to do something. One can tell by the way he talks. You should begin right away. You've wasted too much time already."

Poor Freckles hung his head. He never had wasted an hour in his life. There never had been one that was his to waste.

The Angel, studying him intently, read the thought in his face. "Oh, I don't mean that!" she cried, with the frank dismay of sixteen. "Of course, you're not lazy! No one ever would think that from your appearance. It's this I mean: there is something fine, strong, and full of power in your face. There is something you are to do in this world, and no matter how you work at all these other things, or how successfully you do them, it is all wasted until you find the *one thing* that you can do best. If you hadn't a thing in the world to keep you, and could go anywhere you please and do anything you want, what would you do?" persisted the Angel.

"I'd go to Chicago and sing in the First Episcopal choir," answered Freckles promptly.

The Angel dropped on a seat—the hat she had removed and held in her fingers rolled to her feet. "There!" she exclaimed vehemently. "You can see what I'm going to be. Nothing! Absolutely nothing! You can sing? Of course you can sing! It is written all over you."

"Any one with half wit could have seen he could sing, without having to be told," she thought. "It's in the slenderness of his fingers and his quick nervous touch. It is in the brightness of his hair, the fire of his eyes, the breadth of his chest, the muscles of his throat and neck; and above all, it's in every tone of his voice, for even as he speaks it's the sweetest sound I ever heard from the throat of a mortal."

"Will you do something for me?" she asked.

"I'll do anything in the world you want me to," said Freckles largely; "and if I can't do what you want, I'll go to work at once and I'll try 'til I can."

"Good! That's business!" said the Angel. "You go

over there and stand before that hedge and sing something. Just anything you think of first."

Freckles faced the Angel from his banked wall of brown, blue, and crimson, with its background of solid green, and lifting his face to the sky, he sang the first thing that came into his mind. It was a children's song that he had led for the little folks at the Home many times, recalled to his mind by the Angel's exclamation:

"To fairy-land we go,
With a song of joy, heigh-o:
In dreams we'll stand upon that shore
And all the realm behold;
We'll see the sights so grand
That belong to fairy-land,
Its mysteries we will explore,
Its beauties will unfold.
Oh, tra, la, la, oh, ha, ha, ha! We're happy now as we can be,
Our welcome song we will prolong, and greet you with our melody.
O, fairy-land, sweet fairy-land, we love to sing——"

No song could have given the intense sweetness and rollicking quality of Freckles' voice better scope. He forgot everything but pride in his work. He was singing the chorus, and the Angel was shivering in ecstasy, when clip! clip! came the sharply beating feet of a swiftly ridden horse down the trail from the north. They both sprang toward the entrance.

"Freckles! Freckles!" called the voice of the Bird Woman.

They were at the trail on the instant.

"Both those revolvers loaded?" she asked.

"Yes," said Freckles.

"Is there a way you can cut across the swamp and reach the chicken tree in a few minutes, and with little noise?"

"Yes."

"Then go flying," said the Bird Woman. "Give the Angel a lift behind me, and we will ride the horse back where you left him and wait for you. I finished Little Chicken in no time and put him back. His mother came so close, I felt sure she would enter the log. The light was fine, so I set and focussed the camera and covered it with branches, attached the long hose, and went away over a hundred feet and hid in some bushes to wait. A short, stout man and a tall, dark one passed me so closely I almost could have reached out and touched them. They carried a big saw on their shoulders. They said they could work until near noon, and then they must lay off until you passed and then try to load and get out at night. They went on—not entirely from sight—and began cutting a tree. Mr. McLean told me the other day what would probably happen here, and if they fell that tree he loses his wager on you. Keep to the east and north and hustle. We'll meet you at the carriage. I always am armed. Give Angel one of your revolvers, and you keep the other. We will separate and creep toward them from different sides and give them a fusillade that will send them flying. You hurry, now!"

She lifted the reins and started briskly down the trail. The Angel, hatless and with sparkling eyes, was clinging around her waist.

Freckles wheeled and ran. He worked his way with

much care, dodging limbs and bushes with noiseless tread, and cutting as closely where he thought the men were as he felt that he dared if he were to remain unseen. As he ran he tried to think. It was Wessner, burning for his revenge, aided by the bully of the locality, that he was going to meet. He was accustomed to that thought but not to the complication of having two women on his hands who undoubtedly would have to be taken care of in spite of the Bird Woman's offer to help him. His heart was jarring as it never had before with running. He must follow the Bird Woman's plan and meet them at the carriage, but if they really did intend to try to help him, he must not allow it. Allow the Angel to try to handle a revolver in his defence? Never! Not for all the trees in the Limberlost! She might shoot herself. She might forget to watch sharply and run across a snake that was not particularly well behaved that morning. Freckles permitted himself a grim smile as he went speeding on.

When he reached the carriage, the Bird Woman and the Angel had the horse hitched, the outfit packed, and were calmly waiting. The Bird Woman held a revolver in her hand. She wore dark clothing. They had pinned a big focussing cloth over the front of the Angel's light dress.

"Give Angel one of your revolvers, quick!" said the Bird Woman. "We will creep up until we are in fair range. The underbrush is so thick and they are so busy that they will never notice us, if we don't make a noise. You fire first, then I will pop in from my direction, and then you, Angel, and shoot quite high, or else very low. We mustn't really hit them. We'll go close enough to the cowards to make it interesting, and keep it up until we have them going."

Freckles protested.

The Bird Woman reached over, and, taking the smaller revolver from his belt, handed it to the Angel. "Keep your nerve steady, dear; watch where you step, and shoot high," she said. "Go straight at them from where you are. Wait until you hear Freckles' first shot, then follow me as closely as you can, to let them know that we outnumber them. If you want to save McLean's wager on you, now you go!" she commanded Freckles, who, with an agonized glance at the Angel, ran toward the east.

The Bird Woman chose the middle distance, and for a last time cautioned the Angel as she moved away to lie down and shoot high.

Through the underbrush the Bird Woman crept even more closely than she had intended, found a clear range, and waited for Freckles' shot. There was one long minute of sickening suspense. The men straightened for breath. Work was difficult with a hand-saw in the heat of the swamp. As they rested, the big dark fellow took a bottle from his pocket and began oiling the saw.

"We got to keep mighty quiet," he said, "and wait to fell it until that damned guard has gone to his dinner."

Again they bent to their work. Freckles' revolver spat fire. Lead spanged on steel. The saw-handle flew from Wessner's hand and he reeled from the jar of the shock. Black Jack straightened, uttering a fearful oath. The hat sailed from his head from the far northeast. The Angel had not waited for the Bird Woman, and her shot scarcely could have been called high. At almost the same instant the third shot whistled from the east. Black Jack sprang into the air with a yell of complete panic, for it ripped a heel from his boot. Freckles emptied his second chamber, and the earth spattered over Wessner. Shots poured in rapidly. Without even reaching for a weapon, both men ran toward the east road in great leaping bounds, while leaden slugs sung and hissed around them in deadly earnest.

Freckles was trimming his corners as closely as he dared, but if the Angel did not really intend to hit, she was taking risks in a scandalous manner.

When the men reached the trail, Freckles yelled at the top of his voice: "Head them off on the south, boys! Fire from the south!"

As he had hoped, Jack and Wessner instantly plunged into the swale. A spattering of lead followed them. They crossed the swale, running low, with not even one backward glance, and entered the woods beyond the corduroy.

Then the little party gathered at the tree.

"I'd better fix this saw so they can't be using it if they come back," said Freckles, taking out his hatchet and making saw-teeth fly.

"Now we must leave here without being seen," said the Bird Woman to the Angel. "It won't do for me to make enemies of these men, for I am likely to meet them while at work any day."

"You can do it by driving straight north on this road," said Freckles. "I will go ahead and cut the wires for you. The swale is almost dry. You will only be sinking a little. In a few rods you will strike a corn-field. I will take down the fence and let you into that. Follow the furrows and drive straight across it until you come to the other side. Be following the fence south until you come to a road through the woods east of it. Then take that road and follow east until you reach the pike. You will come out on your way back to town, and two miles north of anywhere they are likely to be. Don't for your lives ever let it out that you did this," he earnestly cautioned, "for it's black enemies you would be making."

Freckles clipped the wires and they drove through. The Angel leaned from the carriage and held out his revolver. Freckles looked at her in surprise. Her eyes were black, while her face was a deeper rose than usual. He felt that his own was white.

"Did I shoot high enough?" she asked sweetly. "I really forgot about lying down."

Freckles winced. Did the child know how close she had gone? Surely she could not! Or was it possible that she had the nerve and skill to fire like that purposely?

"I will send the first reliable man I meet for McLean," said the Bird Woman, gathering up the lines. "If I don't meet one when we reach town, we will send a messenger. If it wasn't for having the gang see me, I would go myself; but I will promise you that you will have help in a little over two hours. You keep well hidden. They must think some of the gang is with you now. There isn't a chance that they will be back, but don't run any risks. Remain under cover. If they should come, it probably would be for their saw." She laughed as at a fine joke.

CHAPTER VII

Wherein Freckles Wins Honour and Finds a Footprint on the Trail

CHAPTER VII

Wherein Freckles Wins Honour and Finds a Footprint on the Trail

ROUND-EYED, Freckles watched the Bird Woman and the Angel drive away. After they were from sight and he was safely hidden among the branches of a small tree, he remembered that he neither had thanked them nor said good-bye. Considering what they had been through, they never would come again. His heart sank until he had palpitation in his wading-boots.

Stretching the length of the limb, he thought deeply, though he was not thinking of Black Jack or Wessner. Would the Bird Woman and the Angel come again? No other woman whom he ever had known would. But did they resemble any other women he ever had known? He thought of the Bird Woman's unruffled face and the Angel's revolver practice, and presently he was not so sure that they would not return.

What were the people in the big world like? His knowledge was so very limited. There had been people at the Home, who exchanged a stilted, perfunctory kindness for their salaries. The visitors who called on receiving days he had divided into three classes: the psalm-singing kind, who came with a tear in the eye and hypocrisy in every feature of their faces; the kind who dressed in silks and jewels, and handed to those poor, little mother-hungry souls worn toys that their children no longer cared for, in exactly the same spirit in which they pitched biscuits to the monkeys at the "zoo," and for the same reason—to see how they would take them and be amused by what they would do; and the third class, whom he considered real people. They made him feel they cared that he was there, and that they would have been glad to see him elsewhere.

Now here was another class, that had all they needed of the world's best and were engaged in doing work that counted. They had things worth while to be proud of; and they had met him as a son and brother. With them he could, for the only time in his life, forget the lost hand that every day tortured him with a new pang. What kind of people were they and where did they belong among the classes he knew? He failed to decide, because he never had known others similar to them; but how he loved them!

In the world where he was going soon, were the majority like them, or were they of the hypocrite and bun-throwing classes?

He had forgotten the excitement of the morning and the passing of time when distant voices aroused him, and he gently lifted his head. Nearer and nearer they came, and as the heavy wagons rumbled down the east trail he could hear them plainly. The gang were shouting themselves hoarse for the Limberlost Guard. Freckles did not feel that he deserved it. He would have given much to be able to go to the men and explain, but to McLean only could he tell his story.

At the sight of Freckles the men threw up their hats and cheered. McLean shook hands with him warmly, but big Duncan gathered him into his arms and hugged him as a bear and choked over a few words of praise. The gang drove in and finished felling the tree. McLean was angry beyond measure at this attempt on his property, for in their haste to fell the tree the thieves had cut too high and wasted a foot and a half of valuable timber.

When the last wagon rolled away, McLean sat on the stump and Freckles told the story he was aching to tell. The Boss scarcely could believe his senses. Also, he was much disappointed.

"I have been almost praying all the way over, Freckles," he said, "that you would have some evidence by which we could arrest those fellows and get them out of our way, but this will never do. We can't mix up those women in it. They have helped you save me the tree and my wager as well. Going across the country as she does, the Bird Woman never could be expected to testify against them."

"No, indeed; nor the Angel, either, sir," said Freckles.

"The Angel?" queried the astonished McLean.

The Boss listened in silence while Freckles told of the coming and christening of the Angel.

"I know her father well," said McLean at last, "and I have often seen her. You are right; she is a beautiful young girl, and she appears to be utterly free from the least particle of false pride or foolishness. I do not understand why her father risks such a jewel in this place."

"He's daring it because she is a jewel, sir," said Freckles, eagerly. "Why, she's trusting a rattlesnake to rattle before it strikes her, and of course, she thinks she can trust mankind as well. The man isn't made who wouldn't lay down the life of him for her. She doesn't need any care. Her face and the pretty ways of her are all the protection she would need in a band of howling savages."

"Did you say she handled one of the revolvers?" asked McLean.

"She scared all the breath out of me body," admitted Freckles. "Seems that her father has taught her to shoot. The Bird Woman told her distinctly to lie low and blaze away high, just to help scare them. The spunky little thing followed them right out into the west road, spitting lead like hail, and clipping all around the heads and heels of them; and I'm damned, sir, if I believe she'd cared a rap if she'd hit. I never saw much shooting, but if that wasn't the nearest to miss I ever want to see! Scared the life near out of me body with the fear that she'd drop one of them. As long as I'd no one to help me but a couple of women that didn't dare be mixed up in it, all I could do was to let them get away."

"Now, will they come back?" asked McLean.

"Of course!" said Freckles. "They're not going to be taking that. You could stake your life on it, they'll be coming back. At least, Black Jack will. Wessner may not have the pluck, unless he is half drunk. Then he'd be a terror. And the next time——" Freckles hesitated.

"What?"

"It will be a question of who shoots first and straightest."

"Then the only thing for me to do is to double the guard and bring the gang here the first minute possible.

As soon as I feel that we have the rarest of the stuff out below, we will come. The fact is, in many cases, until it is felled it's difficult to tell what a tree will prove to be. It won't do to leave you here longer alone. Jack has been shooting twenty years to your one, and it stands to reason that you are no match for him. Who of the gang would you like best to have with you?"

"No one, sir," said Freckles, emphatically. "Next time is where I run. I won't try to fight them alone. I'll just be getting wind of them, and then make tracks for you. I'll need to come like lightning, and Duncan has no extra horse, so I'm thinking you'd best get me one—or perhaps a wheel would be better. I used to do extra work for the Home doctor, and he would let me take his bicycle to ride around the place. And at times the head nurse would loan me his for an hour. A wheel would cost less and be faster than a horse, and would take less care. I believe, if you are going to town soon, you had best pick up any kind of an old one at some second-hand store, for if I'm ever called to use it in a hurry there won't be the handlebars left after crossing the corduroy."

"Yes," said McLean; "and if you didn't have a first-class wheel, you never could cross the corduroy on it at all."

As they walked to the cabin, McLean insisted on another guard, but Freckles was stubbornly set on fighting his battle alone. He made one mental condition. If the Bird Woman was going to give up the Little Chicken series, he would yield to the second guard, solely for the sake of her work and the presence of the Angel in the Limberlost. He did not propose to have a second man unless it were absolutely necessary, for he had been alone so long that he loved the solitude, his chickens, and flowers. The thought of having a stranger to all his ways come and meddle with his arrangements, frighten his pets, pull his flowers, and interrupt him when he wanted to study, so annoyed him that he was blinded to his real need for help.

With McLean it was a case of letting his sober, better judgment be overridden by the boy he was growing so to love that he could not endure to oppose him, and to have Freckles keep his trust and win alone meant more than any money the Boss might lose.

The following morning McLean brought the wheel, and Freckles took it to the trail to test it. It was new, chainless, with as little as possible to catch in hurried riding, and in every way the best of its kind. Freckles went skimming around the trail on it on a preliminary trip before he locked it in his case and started his minute examination of his line on foot. He glanced around his room as he left it, and then stood staring.

On the moss before his prettiest seat lay the Angel's hat. In the excitement of yesterday all of them had forgotten it. He went and picked it up, oh! so carefully, gazing at it with hungry eyes, but touching it only to carry it to his case, where he hung it on the shining handlebar of the new wheel and locked it among his treasures. Then he went to the trail, with a new expression on his face and a strange throbbing in his heart. He was not in the least afraid of anything that morning. He felt he was the veriest Daniel, but all his lions seemed weak and harmless.

What Black Jack's next move would be he could not

imagine, but that there would be a move of some kind was certain. The big bully was not a man to give up his purpose, or to have the hat swept from his head with a bullet and bear it meekly. Moreover, Wessner would cling to his revenge with a Dutchman's singleness of mind.

Freckles tried to think connectedly, but there were too many places on the trail where the Angel's footprints were yet visible. She had stepped in one mucky spot and left a sharp impression. The afternoon sun had baked it hard, and the horses' hoofs had not obliterated any part of it, as they had in so many places. Freckles stood fascinated, gazing at it. He measured it lovingly with his eye. He would not have ventured a caress on her hat any more than on her person, but this was different. Surely a footprint on a trail might belong to any one who found and wanted it. He stooped under the wires and entered the swamp. With a little searching, he found a big piece of thick bark loose on a log and carefully peeling it, carried it out and covered the print so that the first rain would not obliterate it.

When he reached his room, he tenderly laid the hat upon his book-shelf, and to wear off his awkwardness, mounted his wheel and went spinning on trail again. It was like flying, for the path was worn smooth with his feet and baked hard with the sun almost all the way. When he came to the bark, he veered far to one side and smiled at it in passing. Suddenly he was off the wheel, kneeling beside it. He removed his hat, carefully lifted the bark, and gazed lovingly at the imprint.

"I wonder what she was going to say of me voice," he

whispered. "She never got it said, but from the face of her, I believe she was liking it fairly well. Perhaps she was going to say that singing was the big thing I was to be doing. That's what they all thought at the Home. Well, if it is, I'll just shut me eyes, think of me little room, the face of her watching, and the heart of her beating, and I'll raise them. Damn them, if singing will do it, I'll raise them from the benches!"

With this dire threat, Freckles knelt, as at a wayside spring, and deliberately laid his lips on the footprint. Then he arose, appearing as if he had been drinking at the fountain of gladness.

CHAPTER VIII

Wherein Freckles Meets a Man of Affairs and Loses Nothing by the Encounter

CHAPTER VIII

Wherein Freckles Meets a Man of Affairs and Loses Nothing by the Encounter

"WEEL, I be drawed on!" exclaimed Mrs. Duncan.

Freckles stood before her, holding the Angel's hat.

"I've been thinking this long time that ye or Duncan would see that sunbonnets werena braw enough for a woman of my standing, and ye're a guid laddie to bring me this beautiful hat."

She turned it around, examining the weave of the straw and the foliage trimmings, passing her rough fingers over the satin ties delightedly. As she held it up, admiring it, Freckles' astonished eyes saw a new side of Sarah Duncan. She was jesting, but under the jest the fact loomed strong that, though poor, overworked, and with none but God-given refinement, there was something in her soul crying after that bit of feminine finery, and it made his heart ache for her. He resolved that when he reached the city he would send her a hat, if it took fifty dollars to do it.

She lingeringly handed it back to him.

"It's unco guid of ye to think of me," she said lightly, "but I maun question your taste a wee. D'ye no think ye had best return this and get a woman with half her hair gray a little plainer head-dress? Seems like that's far ower gay for me. I'm no' saying that it's no' exactly what I'd like to hae, but I mauna mak mysel' ridiculous. Ye'd best give this to somebody young and pretty, say about sixteen. Where did ye come by it, Freckles? If there's anything been dropping lately, ye hae forgotten to mention it."

"Do you see anything heavenly about that hat?" queried Freckles, holding it up.

The morning breeze waved the ribbons gracefully, binding one around Freckles' sleeve and the other across his chest, where they caught and clung as if magnetized.

"Yes," said Sarah Duncan. "It's verra plain and simple, but it juist makes ye feel that it's all of the finest stuff. It's exactly what I'd call a heavenly hat."

"Sure," said Freckles, "for it's belonging to an Angel!"

Then he told her about the hat and asked her what he should do with it.

"Take it to her, of course!" said Sarah Duncan. "Like it's the only ane she has and she may need it badly."

Freckles smiled. He had a clear idea about the hat being the only one the Angel had. However, there was a thing he felt he should do and wanted to do, but he was not sure.

"You think I might be taking it home?" he said.

"Of course ye must," said Mrs. Duncan. "And without another hour's delay. It's been here two days noo, and she may want it, and be too busy or afraid to come."

"But how can I take it?" asked Freckles.

"Gang spinning on your wheel. Ye can do it easy in an hour."

"But in that hour, what if——?"

"Nonsense!" interrupted Sarah Duncan. "Ye've watched that timber-line until ye're grown fast to it, lad. Give me your boots and club and I'll gae walk the south end and watch doon the east and west sides until ye come back."

"Mrs. Duncan! You never would be doing it," cried Freckles.

"Why not?" inquired she.

"But you know you're mortal afraid of snakes and a lot of other things in the swamp."

"I am afraid of snakes," said Mrs. Duncan, "but likely they've gone into the swamp this hot weather. I'll juist stay on the trail and watch, and ye might hurry the least bit. The day's so bright it feels like storm. I can put the bairns on the woodpile to play until I get back. Ye gang awa and take the blessed little angel her beautiful hat."

"Are you sure it will be all right?" urged Freckles. "Do you think if Mr. McLean came he would care?"

"Na," said Mrs. Duncan; "I dinna. If ye and me agree that a thing ought to be done, and I watch in your place, why, it's bound to be all right with McLean. Let me pin the hat in a paper, and ye jump on your wheel and gang flying. Ought ye put on your Sabbath-day clothes?"

Freckles shook his head. He knew what he should do, but there was no use in taking time to try to explain it to Mrs. Duncan while he was so hurried. He exchanged his wading-boots for shoes, gave her his club, and went spinning toward town. He knew very well where the Angel lived. He had seen her home many times, and he passed it again without even raising his eyes from the street, steering straight for her father's place of business.

Carrying the hat, Freckles passed a long line of clerks, and at the door of the private office asked to see the proprietor. When he had waited a moment, a tall, spare, keen-eyed man faced him, and in brisk, nervous tones asked: "How can I serve you, sir?"

Freckles handed him the package and answered, "By delivering to your daughter this hat, which she was after leaving at me place the other day, when she went away in a hurry. And by saying to her and the Bird Woman that I'm more thankful than I'll be having words to express for the brave things they was doing for me. I'm McLean's Limberlost guard, sir."

"Why don't you take it yourself?" questioned the Man of Affairs.

Freckles' clear gray eyes met those of the Angel's father squarely, and he asked: "If you were in my place, would you take it to her yourself?"

"No, I would not," said that gentleman quickly.

"Then why ask why I did not?" came Freckles' lamb-like query.

"Bless me!" said the Angel's father. He stared at the package, then at the lifted chin of the boy, and then at the package again, and muttered, "Excuse me!"

Freckles bowed.

"It would be favouring me greatly if you would deliver

the hat and the message. Good-morning, sir," and he turned away.

"One minute," said the Angel's father. "Suppose I give you permission to return this hat in person and make your own acknowledgments."

Freckles stood one moment thinking intently, and then he lifted those eyes of unswerving truth and asked: "Why should you, sir? You are kind, indade, to mention it, and it's thanking you I am for your good intintions, but my wanting to go or your being willing to have me ain't proving that your daughter would be wanting me or care to bother with me."

The Angel's father looked keenly into the face of this extraordinary young man, for he found it to his liking.

"There's one other thing I meant to say," said Freckles. "Every day I see something, and at times a lot of things, that I think the Bird Woman would be wanting pictures of badly, if she knew. You might be speaking of it to her, and if she'd want me to, I can send her word when I find things she wouldn't likely get elsewhere."

"If that's the case," said the Angel's father, "and you feel under obligations for her assistance the other day, you can discharge them in that way. She is spending all her time in the fields and woods searching for subjects. If you run across things, perhaps rarer than she may find, about your work, it would save her the time she spends searching for subjects, and she could work in security under your protection. By all means let her know if you find subjects you think she could use, and we will do anything we can for you, if you will give her what help you can and see that she is as safe as possible."

"It's hungry for human beings I am," said Freckles, "and it's like Heaven to me to have them come. Of course, I'll be telling or sending her word every time me work can spare me. Anything I can do it would make me uncommon happy, but"—again truth had to be told, because it was Freckles who was speaking—"when it comes to protecting them, I'd risk me life, to be sure, but even that mightn't do any good in some cases. There are many dangers to be reckoned with in the swamp, sir, that call for every person to look sharp. If there wasn't really thieving to guard against, why, McLean wouldn't need be paying out good money for a guard. I'd love them to be coming, and I'll do all I can, but you must be told that there's danger of them running into timber-thieves again any day, sir."

"Yes," said the Angel's father, "and I suppose there's danger of the earth opening up and swallowing the town any day, but I'm damned if I quit business for fear it will, and the Bird Woman won't, either. Every one knows her and her work, and there is no danger in the world of any one in any way molesting her, even if he were stealing a few of McLean's gold-plated trees. She's as safe in the Limberlost as she is at home, so far as timber-thieves are concerned. All I am ever uneasy about are the snakes, poison-vines, and insects; and those are risks she must run anywhere. You need not hesitate a minute about that. I shall be glad to tell them what you wish. Thank you very much, and good-day, sir."

There was no way in which Freckles could know it, but by following his best instincts and being what he conceived a gentleman should be, he surprised the Man of Affairs into thinking of him and seeing his face over his books many times that morning; whereas, if he had gone to the Angel as he had longed to do, her father never would have given him a second thought.

On the street he drew a deep breath. How had he acquitted himself? He only knew that he had lived up to his best impulse, and that is all any one can do. He glanced over his wheel to see that it was all right, and just as he stepped to the curb to mount he heard a voice that thrilled him through and through: "Freckles! Oh Freckles!"

The Angel separated from a group of laughing sweet-faced girls and came hurrying to him. She was in snowy white—a quaint little frock, with a marvel of soft lace around her throat and wrists. Through the sheer sleeves of it her beautiful, rounded arms showed distinctly, and it was cut just to the base of her perfect neck. On her head was a pure white creation of fancy braid, with folds on folds of tulle, soft and silken as cobwebs, lining the brim; while a mass of white roses clustered against the gold of her hair, crept around the crown, and fell in a riot to her shoulders at the back. There were gleams of gold with settings of blue on her fingers, and altogether she was the daintiest, sweetest sight he ever had seen. Freckles, standing on the curb, forgot himself in his cotton shirt, corduroys, and his belt to which his wire-cutter and pliers were hanging, and gazed as a man gazes when first he sees the woman he adores with all her charms enhanced by appropriate and beautiful clothing.

"Oh Freckles," she cried as she came to him. "I was wondering about you the other day. Do you know I never saw you in town before. You watch that old line so closely! Why did you come? Is there any trouble? Are you just starting to the Limberlost?"

"I came to bring your hat," said Freckles. "You forgot it in the rush the other day. I have left it with your father, and a message trying to ixpriss the gratitude of me for how you and the Bird Woman were for helping me out."

The Angel nodded gravely, then Freckles saw that he had done the proper thing in going to her father. His heart bounded until it jarred his body, for she was saying that she scarcely could wait for the time to come for the next picture of the Little Chicken series. "I want to hear the remainder of that song, and I hadn't even begun seeing your room yet," she complained. "As for singing, if you can sing like that every day, I never can get enough of it. I wonder if I couldn't bring my banjo and some of the songs I like best. I'll play and you sing, and we'll put the birds out of commission."

Freckles stood on the curb with drooped eyes, for he felt that if he lifted them the tumult of tender adoration in them would show and frighten her.

"I was afraid your ixperience the other day would scare you so that you'd never be coming again," he found himself saying.

The Angel laughed gaily.

"Did I seem scared?" she questioned.

"No," said Freckles; "you did not."

"Oh, I just enjoyed that," she cried. "Those hateful, stealing old things! I had a big notion to pink one of them, but I thought maybe someway it would be best for you that I shouldn't. They needed it. That didn't scare me; and as for the Bird Woman, she's accustomed to finding snakes, tramps, cross dogs, sheep, cattle, and goodness knows what! You can't frighten her when she's after a picture. Did they come back?"

"No," said Freckles. "The gang got there a little after noon and took out the tree, but I must tell you, and you must tell the Bird Woman, that there's no doubt but they will be coming back, and they will have to make it before long now, for it's soon the gang will be there to work on the swamp."

"Oh, what a shame!" cried the Angel. "They'll clear out roads, cut down the beautiful trees, and tear up everything. They'll drive away the birds and spoil the cathedral. When they have done their worst, then all these mills close here will follow in and take out the cheap timber. Then the landowners will dig a few ditches, build some fires, and in two summers more the Limberlost will be in corn and potatoes."

They looked at each other, and groaned despairingly in unison.

"You like it, too," said Freckles.

"Yes," said the Angel; "I love it. Your room is a little piece right out of the heart of fairy-land, and the cathedral is God's work, not yours. You only found it and opened the door after He had it completed. The birds, flowers, and vines are all so lovely. The Bird Woman says it is really a fact that the mallows, foxfire, iris, and lilies are larger and of richer colouring there than in the remainder of the country. She says it's because of the rich loam and muck. I hate seeing the swamp torn up, and to you it will be like losing your best friend; won't it?"

"Something like," said Freckles. "Still, I've the Limberlost in me heart so that all of it will be real to me while I live, no matter what they do to it. I'm glad past telling if you will be coming a few more times, at least until the gang arrives. Past that time I don't allow mesilf to be thinking."

"Come, have a cool drink before you start back," said the Angel.

"I couldn't possibly," said Freckles. "I left Mrs. Duncan on the trail, and she's terribly afraid of a lot of things. If she even sees a big snake, I don't know what she'll do."

"It won't take but a minute, and you can ride fast enough to make up for it. Please. I want to think of something fine for you, to make up a little for what you did for me that first day."

Freckles looked in sheer wonderment into the beautiful face of the Angel. Did she truly mean it? Would she walk down that street with him, crippled, homely, in mean clothing, with the tools of his occupation on him, and share with him the treat she was offering? He could not believe it, even of the Angel. Still, in justice to the candour of her pure, sweet face, he would not think that she would make the offer and not mean it. She really did mean just what she said, but when it came to carrying out her offer and he saw the stares of her friends, the sneers of her enemies—if such as she could have enemies—and heard the whispered jeers of the curious, then she would see her mistake and be sorry. It would be only a manly thing for him to think this out, and save her from the results of her own blessed bigness of heart.

"I railly must be off," said Freckles earnestly, "but I'm thanking you more than you'll ever know for your kindness. I'll just be drinking bowls of icy things all me way home in the thoughts of it."

Down came the Angel's foot. Her eyes flashed indignantly. "There's no sense in that," she said. "How do you think you would have felt when you knew I was warm and thirsty and you went and brought me a drink and I wouldn't take it because—because goodness knows why! You can ride faster to make up for the time. I've just thought out what I want to fix for you."

She stepped to his side and deliberately slipped her hand under his arm—that right arm that ended in an empty sleeve.

"You are coming," she said firmly. "I won't have it."

Freckles could not have told how he felt, neither could any one else. His blood rioted and his head swam, but he kept his wits. He bent over her.

"Please don't, Angel," he said softly. "You don't understand."

How Freckles came to understand was a problem.

"It's this," he persisted. "If your father met me on the street, in my station and dress, with you on me arm, he'd have every right to be caning me before the people, and not a finger would I lift to stay him."

The Angel's eyes snapped. "If you think my father cares about my doing anything that is right and kind, and that makes me happy to do—why, then you completely failed in reading my father, and I'll ask him and just show you."

She dropped Freckles' arm and turned toward the entrance to the building. "Why, look there!" she exclaimed.

Her father stood in a big window fronting the street, a bundle of papers in his hand, interestedly watching the little scene, with eyes that comprehended quite as thoroughly as if he had heard every word. The Angel caught his glance and made a despairing little gesture toward Freckles. The Man of Affairs answered her with a look of infinite tenderness. He nodded his head and waved the papers in the direction she had indicated, and the veriest dolt could have read the words his lips formed: "Take him along!"

A sudden trembling seized Freckles. At sight of the Angel's father he had stepped back as far from her as he could, leaned the wheel against him, and snatched off his hat.

The Angel turned on him with triumphing eyes.

She was highly strung and not accustomed to being thwarted. "Did you see that?" she demanded. "Now are you satisfied? Will you come, or must I call a policeman to bring you?"

Freckles went. There was nothing else to do. Guiding

his wheel, he walked down the street beside her. On every hand she was kept busy giving and receiving the cheeriest greetings. She walked into the parlours exactly as if she owned them. A clerk came hurrying to meet her.

"There's a table vacant beside a window where it is cool. I'll save it for you," and he started back.

"Please not," said the Angel. "I've taken this man unawares, when he's in a rush. I'm afraid if we sit down we'll take too much time and afterward he will blame me."

She walked to the fountain, and a long row of people stared with all the varying degrees of insolence and curiosity that Freckles had felt they would. He glanced at the Angel. *Now* would she see?

"On my soul!" he muttered under his breath. "They don't aven touch her!"

She laid down her sunshade and gloves. She walked to the end of the counter and turned the full battery of her eyes on the attendant.

"Please," she said.

The white-aproned individual stepped back and gave delighted assent. The Angel stepped beside him, and selecting a tall, flaring glass, of almost paper thinness, she stooped and rolled it in a tray of cracked ce.

"I want to mix a drink for my friend," she said. "He has a long, hot ride before him, and I don't want him started off with one of those old palate-teasing sweetnesses that you mix just on purpose to drive a man back in ten minutes." There was an appreciative laugh from the line at the counter.

"I want a clear, cool, sparkling drink that has a tang of

acid in it. Where's the cherry phosphate? That, not at all sweet, would be good; don't you think?"

The attendant did think. He pointed out the different taps, and the Angel compounded the drink, while Freckles, standing so erect he almost leaned backward, gazed at her and paid no attention to any one else. When she had the glass brimming, she tilted a little of its contents into a second glass and tasted it.

"That's entirely too sweet for a thirsty man," she said.

She poured out half the mixture, and refilling the glass, tasted it a second time. She submitted that result to the attendant. "Isn't that about the thing?" she asked.

He replied enthusiastically: "I'd get my wages raised ten a month if I could learn that trick."

The Angel carried the brimming, frosty glass to Freckles. He removed his hat, and lifting the icy liquid even with her eyes and looking straight into them, he said in the mellowest of all the mellow tones of his voice: "I'll be drinking it to the Swamp Angel."

As he had said to her that first day, she now cautioned him: "Be drinking slowly."

When the screen-door swung behind them, one of the men at the cou ter asked of the attendant: "Now, what did that mean? '

"Exactly what you saw," replied he, rather curtly. "We're accustomed to it here. Hardly a day passes, this hot weather, but she's picking up some poor, god-forsaken mortal and bringing him in. Then she comes behind the counter herself and fixes up a drink to suit the occasion. She's all sorts of fancies about what's what for all kinds of times and conditions, and you bet she can just hit the spot! Ain't a clerk here can put up a drink to touch her. She's a sort of knack at it. Every once in a while, when the Boss sees her, he calls out to her to mix him a drink."

"And does she?" asked the man with an interested grin.

"Well, I guess! But first she goes back and sees how long it is since he's had a drink. What he drank last. How warm he is. When he ate last. Then she comes here and mixes a glass of fizz with a little touch of acid, and a bit of cherry, lemon, grape, pineapple, or something sour and cooling, and it hits the spot just as no spot was ever hit before. I honestly believe that the *interest* she takes in it is half the trick, for I watch her closely and I can't come within gun-shot of her concoctions. She has a running bill here. Her father settles once a month. She gives nine-tenths of it away. Hardly ever touches it herself, but when she does she makes me mix it. She's just old persimmons. Even the scrub-boy of this establishment would fight for her. It lasts the year round, for in winter it's some poor, frozen cuss that she's warming up on hot coffee or chocolate."

"Mighty queer specimen she had this time," volunteered another. "Irish, hand off, straight as a ramrod, and something worth while in his face. Notice that hat peel off, and the eyes of him? There's a case of 'fight for her!' Wonder who he is?"

"I think," said a third, "that he's McLean's Limberlost guard, and I suspect she's gone to the swamp with the

Bird Woman for pictures and knows him that way. I've heard that he is a master hand with the birds, and that would just suit the Bird Woman to a T."

On the street the Angel walked beside Freckles to the first crossing and there she stopped. "Now, will you promise to ride fast enough to make up for the five minutes that took?" she asked. "I am a little uneasy about Mrs. Duncan."

Freckles turned his wheel into the street. It seemed to him he had poured that delicious icy liquid into every vein in his body instead of his stomach. It even went to his brain.

"Did you insist on fixing that drink because you knew how intoxicating 'twould be?" he asked.

There was subtlety in the compliment and it delighted the Angel. She laughed gleefully.

"Next time, maybe you won't take so much coaxing," she teased.

"I wouldn't this, if I had known your father and been understanding you better. Do you really think the Bird Woman will be coming again?"

The Angel jeered. "Wild horses couldn't drag her away," she cried. "She will have hard work to wait the week out. I shouldn't be in the least surprised to see her start any hour."

Freckles could not endure the suspense; it had to come.

"And you?" he questioned, but he dared not lift his eyes.

"Wild horses me, too," she laughed, "couldn't keep me away either! I dearly love to come, and the next time I am going to bring my banjo, and I'll play, and you sing for me some of the songs I like best; won't you?"

"Yis," said Freckles, because it was all he was capable of saying just then.

"It's beginning to act stormy," she said. "If you hurry you will just about make it. Now, good-bye."

CHAPTER IX

Wherein the Limberlost Falls upon Mrs. Duncan and Freckles Comes to the Rescue

CHAPTER IX

Wherein the Limberlost Falls upon Mrs. Duncan and Freckles Comes to the Rescue

FRECKLES was half-way to the Limberlost when he dismounted. He could ride no farther, because he could not see the road. He sat under a tree, and, leaning against it, sobs shook, twisted, and rent him. If they would remind him of his position, speak condescendingly, or notice his hand, he could endure it, but this—it surely would kill him! His hot, pulsing Irish blood was stirred deeply. What did they mean? Why did they do it? Were they like that to every one? Was it pity?

It could not be, for he knew that the Bird Woman and the Angel's father must know that he was not really McLean's son, and it did not matter to them in the least. In spite of accident and poverty, they evidently expected him to do something worth while in the world. That must be his remedy. He must work on his education. He must get away. He must find and do the great thing of which the Angel talked. For the first time, his thoughts turned anxiously toward the city and the beginning of his studies. McLean and the Duncans spoke of him as "the boy," but he was a man. He must face life bravely and act a man's part. The Angel was a mere child. He must not allow her to torture him past endurance with her frank comradeship that meant to him high heaven, earth's richness, and all that lay between, and *nothing* to her.

There was an ominous growl of thunder, and amazed at himself, Freckles snatched up his wheel and raced toward the swamp. He was worried to find his boots lying at the cabin door; the children playing on the wood-pile told him that "mither" said they were so heavy she couldn't walk in them, and she had come back and taken them off. Thoroughly frightened, he stopped only long enough to slip them on, and then sped with all his strength for the Limberlost. To the west, the long, black, hard-beaten trail lay clear; but far up the east side, straight across the path, he could see what was certainly a limp, brown figure. Freckles spun with all his might.

Face down, Sarah Duncan lay across the trail. When Freckles turned her over, his blood chilled at the look of horror settled on her face. There was a low humming and something spatted against him. Glancing around, Freckles shivered in terror, for there was a swarm of wild bees settled on a scrub-thorn only a few yards away. The air was filled with excited, unsettled bees making ready to lead farther in search of a suitable location. Then he thought he understood, and with a prayer of thankfulness in his heart that she had escaped, even so narrowly, he caught her up and hurried down the trail until they were well out of danger. He laid her in the shade, and carrying water from the swamp in the crown of his hat, he bathed her face and hands; but she lay in unbroken stillness, without a sign of life.

She had found Freckles' boots so large and heavy that she had gone back and taken them off, although she was mortally afraid to approach the swamp without them. The thought of it made her nervous, and the fact that she never had been there alone added to her fears. She had not followed the trail many rods when her trouble began. She was not Freckles, so not a bird of the line was going to be fooled into thinking she was.

They began jumping from their nests and darting from unexpected places around her head and feet, with quick whirrs, that kept her starting and dodging. Before Freckles was half-way to the town, poor Mrs. Duncan was hysterical, and the Limberlost had neither sung nor performed for her.

But there was trouble brewing. It was quiet and intensely hot, with that stifling stillness that precedes a summer storm, and feathers and fur were tense and nervous. The birds were singing only a few broken snatches, and flying around, seeking places of shelter. One moment everything seemed devoid of life, the next there was an unexpected whirr, buzz, and sharp cry. Inside, a pandemonium of growling, spatting, snarling, and grunting broke loose.

The swale bent flat before heavy gusts of wind, and the big black chicken swept lower and lower above the swamp. Patches of clouds gathered, shutting out the sun and making it very dark, and the next moment were swept away. The sun poured with fierce, burning brightness, and everything was quiet. It was at the first growl of thunder that Freckles really had noticed the weather, and putting his own troubles aside resolutely, raced for the swamp.

Sarah Duncan paused on the line. "Weel, I wouldna stay in this place for a million a month," she said aloud, and the sound of her voice brought no comfort, for it was so little like she had thought it that she glanced hastily around to see if it had really been she that spoke. She tremblingly wiped the perspiration from her face with the skirt of her sunbonnet.

"Awfu' hot," she panted huskily. "B'lieve there's going to be a big storm. I do hope Freckles will hurry."

Her chin was quivering as a terrified child's. She lifted her bonnet to replace it and brushed against a bush beside her. *Whirr*, almost into her face, went a night-hawk stretched along a limb for its daytime nap. Mrs. Duncan cried out and sprang down the trail, alighting on a frog that was hopping across. The horrible croak it gave as she crushed it sickened her. She screamed wildly and jumped to one side. That carried her into the swale, where the grasses reached almost to her waist, and her horror of snakes returning, she made a flying leap for an old log lying beside the line. She alighted squarely, but it was so damp and rotten that she sank straight through it to her knees. She caught at the wire as she went down, and missing, raked her wrist across a barb until she tore a bleeding gash. Her fingers closed convulsively around the second strand. She was too frightened to scream now. Her tongue stiffened. She clung frantically to the sagging wire, and finally managed to grasp it with the other hand. Then she could reach the top wire, and so she drew herself up and found solid footing. She picked up the club that she had dropped in order to extricate herself. Leaning heavily on it, she managed to return to the trail, but she was trembling so that she scarcely could walk. Going a few steps farther, she came to the stump of the first tree that had been taken out.

She sat bolt upright and very still, trying to collect her thoughts and reason away her terror. A squirrel above her dropped a nut, and as it came rattling down, bouncing from branch to branch, every nerve in her tugged wildly. When the disgusted squirrel barked loudly, she sprang to the trail.

The wind arose higher, the changes from light to darkness were more abrupt, while the thunder came closer and louder at every peal. In swarms the blackbirds arose from the swale and came flocking to the interior, with a clamouring cry: "*T'check, t'check.*" Grackles marshalled to the tribal call: "*Trall-a-hee, trall-a-hee.*" Red-winged blackbirds swept low, calling to belated mates: "*Fol-low-me, fol-low-me.*" Big, jetty crows gathered close to her, crying, as if warning her to flee before it was everlastingly too late. A heron, fishing the near-by pool for Freckles' "find-out" frog, fell into trouble with a muskrat and uttered a rasping note that sent Mrs. Duncan a rod down the line without realizing that she had moved. She was too shaken to run far. She stopped and looked around her fearfully.

Several bees struck her and were angrily buzzing before she noticed them. Then the humming swelled on all sides. A convulsive sob shook her, and she ran into the bushes, now into the swale, anywhere to avoid the swarming bees, ducking, dodging, fighting for her very life. Presently the humming seemed to become a little fainter. She found the trail again, and ran with all her might from a few of her angry pursuers.

As she ran, straining every muscle, she suddenly became aware that, crossing the trail before her, was a big, round, black body, with brown markings on its back, like painted geometrical patterns. She tried to stop, but the louder buzzing behind warned her she dared not. Gathering her skirts higher, with hair flying around her face and her eyes almost bursting from their sockets, she ran straight toward it. The sound of her feet and the humming of the bees alarmed the rattler, so it stopped across the trail, lifting its head above the grasses of the swale and rattling inquiringly, —rattled until the bees were outdone.

Straight toward it went the panic-stricken woman, running wildly and uncontrollably. She took one leap, clearing its body on the path, then flew ahead with winged feet. The snake, coiled to strike, missed Mrs. Duncan and landed among the bees instead. They settled over and around it, and realizing that it had found trouble, it sank among the grasses and went threshing toward its den in the deep willow-fringed low ground. The swale appeared as if a reaper were cutting a wide swath. The mass of enraged bees darted angrily around, searching for it, and striking the scrub-thorn, began a temporary settling there to discover whether it were a suitable place. Completely exhausted, Mrs. Duncan staggered on a few steps farther, fell facing the path, where Freckles found her, and lay quietly.

Freckles worked over her until she drew a long, quivering breath and opened her eyes.

When she saw him bending above her, she closed them tightly, and gripping him, struggled to her feet. He helped her, and with his arm around and half carrying her, they made their way to the clearing. She clung to him with all her remaining strength, but open her eyes she would not until her children came clustering around her. Then, brawny, big Scotswoman though she was, she quietly keeled over again. The children added their wailing to Freckles' panic.

This time he was so close the cabin that he could carry her into the house and lay her on the bed. He sent the oldest boy scudding down the corduroy for the nearest neighbour, and between them they undressed Mrs. Duncan and discovered that she was not bitten. They bathed and bound the bleeding wrist and coaxed her back to consciousness. She lay sobbing and shuddering. The first intelligent word she said was: "Freckles, look at that jar on the kitchen table and see if my yeast is no running ower."

Several days passed before she could give Duncan and Freckles any detailed account of what had happened to her, even then she could not do it without crying as the least of her babies. Freckles was almost heartbroken, and nursed her as well as any woman could have done; while big Duncan, with a heart full for them both, worked early and late to chink every crack of the cabin and examine every spot that possibly could harbour a snake. The effects of her morning on the trail kept her shivering half the time. She could not rest until she sent for McLean and begged him to save Freckles from further risk, in that place of horrors. The Boss went to the swamp with his mind fully determined to do so.

Freckles stood and laughed at him. "Why, Mr. McLean, don't you let a woman's nervous system set you worrying about me," he said. "I'm not denying how she felt, because I've been through it meself, but that's all over and gone: It's the height of me glory to fight it out with the old swamp, and all that's in it, or will be coming to it, and then to turn it over to you as I promised you and meself I'd do, sir. You couldn't break the heart of me entire quicker than to be taking it from me now, when I'm just on the home-stretch. It won't be over three or four weeks yet, and when I've gone it almost a year, why, what's that to me, sir? You mustn't let a woman get mixed up with business, for I've always heard about how it's bringing trouble."

McLean smiled. "What about that last tree?" he said.

Freckles blushed and grinned appreciatively.

"Angels and Bird Women don't count in the common run, sir," he affirmed, shamelessly.

McLean sat in the saddle and laughed.

CHAPTER X

Wherein Freckles Strives Mightily and the Swamp Angel Rewards Him

CHAPTER X

Wherein Freckles Strives Mightily and the Swamp Angel Rewards Him

THE Bird Woman and the Angel did not seem to count in the common run, for they arrived on time for the third of the series and found McLean on the line talking to Freckles. The Boss was filled with enthusiasm over a marsh article of the Bird Woman's that he just had read. He begged to be allowed to accompany her into the swamp and watch the method by which she secured an illustration in such a location.

The Bird Woman explained to him that it was an easy matter with the subject she then had in hand; and as Little Chicken was too small to be frightened by him, and big enough to be growing troublesome, she was glad for his company. They went to the chicken log together, leaving to the happy Freckles the care of the Angel, who had brought her banjo and a roll of songs that she wanted to hear him sing. The Bird Woman told them that they might practise in Freckles' room until she finished with Little Chicken, and then she and McLean would come to the concert.

It was almost three hours before they finished and came down the west trail for their rest and lunch. McLean walked ahead, keeping sharp watch on the trail and clearing it of fallen limbs from overhanging trees. He sent a big piece of bark flying into the swale, and then stopped short and stared at the trail.

The Bird Woman bent forward. Together they studied that imprint of the Angel's foot. At last their eyes met, the Bird Woman's filled with astonishment, and McLean's humid with pity. Neither said a word, but they knew. McLean entered the swale and hunted up the bark. He replaced it, and the Bird Woman carefully stepped over. As they reached the bushes at the entrance, the voice of the Angel stopped them, for it was commanding and filled with much impatience.

"Freckles James Ross McLean!" she was saying, "You fill me with dark-blue despair! You're singing as if your voice were glass and might break at any minute. Why don't you sing as you did a week ago? Answer me that, please."

Freckles smiled confusedly at the Angel, who sat on one of his fancy seats, playing his accompaniment on her banjo.

"You are a fraud," she said. "Here you went last week and led me to think that there was the making of a great singer in you, and now you are singing—do you know how badly you are singing?"

"Yis," said Freckles meekly. "I'm thinking I'm too happy to be singing well to-day. The music don't come right only when I'm lonesome and sad. The world's for being all sunshine at prisint, for among you and Mr. McLean and the Bird Woman I'm after being *that* happy that I can't keep me thoughts on me notes. It's more than sorry I am to be disappointing you. Play it over, and I'll be beginning again, and this time I'll hold hard."

"Well," said the Angel, disgustedly, "it seems to me that if I had all the things to be proud of that you have, I'd lift up my head and sing!"

"And what is it I've to be proud of, ma'am?" politely inquired Freckles.

"Why, a whole worldful of things," cried the Angel, explosively. "For one thing, you can be good and proud over the way you've kept the timber-thieves out of this lease, and the trust your father has in you. You can be proud that you've never even once disappointed him or failed in what he believed you could do. You can be proud over the way every one speaks of you with trust and honour, and about how brave of heart and strong of body you are. I heard a big man say a few days ago that the Limberlost was full of disagreeable things—positive dangers, unhealthful as it could be, and that since the memory of the first settlers it has been a rendezvous for runaways, thieves, and murderers. This swamp is named for a man that was lost here and wandered around 'til he starved. That man I was talking with said he wouldn't take your job for a thousand dollars a month—in fact, he said he wouldn't have it for any money, and you've never missed a day or lost a tree. Proud! Why, I should think you would just parade around about proper over that!

"And you can always be proud that you are born an Irishman. My father is Irish, and if you want to see him get up and strut, give him a teeny opening to enlarge on his race. He says that if the Irish had decent territory they'd lead the world. He says they've always been handicapped by lack of space and of fertile soil. He says if Ireland had been as big and fertile as Indiana, why, England wouldn't ever have had the upper hand. She'd only be an appendage. Fancy England an appendage! He says Ireland has the finest orators and the keenest statesmen in Europe to-day, and when England wants to fight, with whom does she fill her trenches? Irishmen, of course! Ireland has the greenest grass and trees, the finest stones and lakes, and they've jaunting-cars. I don't know just exactly what they are, but Ireland has all there are, anyway. They've a lot of great actors, and a few singers, and there never was a sweeter poet than one of theirs. You should hear my father recite 'Dear Harp of My Country.' He does it this way."

The Angel arose, made an elaborate old-time bow, and holding up the banjo, recited in clipping feet and metre, with rhythmic swing and a touch of brogue that was simply irresistible:

"Dear harp of my country" [The Angel ardently clasped the banjo],

"In darkness I found thee" [She held it to the light],

"The cold chain of silence had hung o'er thee long" [She muted the strings with her rosy palm];

"Then proudly, my own Irish harp, I unbound thee" [She threw up her head and swept a ringing harmony];

"And gave all thy chords to light, freedom, and song" [She crashed into the notes of the accompaniment she had been playing for Freckles].

"That's what you want to be thinking of!" she cried.

"Not darkness, and lonesomeness, and sadness, but 'light, freedom, and song.' I can't begin to think off-hand of all the big, splendid things an Irishman has to be proud of; but whatever they are, they are all yours, and you are a part of them. I just despise that 'saddest-when-I-sing' business. You can sing! Now you go over there and do it! Ireland has had her statesmen, warriors, actors, and poets; now you be her voice! You stand right out there before the cathedral door, and I'm going to come down the aisle playing that accompaniment, and when I stop in front of you—you sing!"

The Angel's face wore an unusual flush. Her eyes were flashing and she was palpitating with earnestness.

She parted the bushes and disappeared. Freckles, straight and tense, stood waiting. Presently, before he saw she was there, she was coming down the aisle toward him, playing compellingly, and rifts of light were touching her with golden glory. Freckles stood as if transfixed.

The cathedral was majestically beautiful, from arched dome of frescoed gold, green, and blue in never-ending shades and harmonies, to the mosaic aisle she trod, richly inlaid in choicest colours, and gigantic pillars that were God's handiwork fashioned and perfected through ages of sunshine and rain. But the fair young face and divinely moulded form of the Angel were His most perfect work of all. Never had she appeared so surpassingly beautiful. She was smiling encouragingly now, and as she came toward him, she struck the chords full and strong.

The heart of poor Freckles almost burst with dull pain and his great love for her. In his desire to fulfil her expectations he forgot everything else, and when she reached his initial chord he was ready. He literally burst forth:

> "Three little leaves of Irish green,
>   United on one stem,
> Love, truth, and valour do they mean,
>   They form a magic gem."

The Angel's eyes widened curiously and her lips parted. A deep colour swept into her cheeks. She had intended to arouse him. She had more than succeeded. She was too young to know that in the effort to rouse a man, women frequently kindle fires that they neither can quench nor control. Freckles was looking over her head now and singing that song, as it never had been sung before, for her alone; and instead of her helping him, as she had intended, he was carrying her with him on the waves of his voice, away, away into another world. When he struck into the chorus, wide-eyed and panting, she was swaying toward him and playing with all her might.

> "Oh, do you love? Oh, say you love
> You love the shamrock green!"

At the last note, Freckles' voice ceased and he looked at the Angel. He had given his best and his all. He fell on his knees and folded his arms across his breast. The Angel, as if magnetized, walked straight down the aisle to him, and running her fingers into the crisp masses of his red hair, tilted his head back and laid her lips on his forehead.

Then she stepped back and faced him. "Good boy!"

she said, in a voice that wavered from the throbbing of her shaken heart. "Dear boy! I knew you could do it! I knew it was in you! Freckles, when you go into the world, if you can face a big audience and sing like that, just once, you will be immortal, and anything you want will be yours."

"Anything!" gasped Freckles.

"Anything," said the Angel.

Freckles arose, muttered something, and catching up his old bucket, plunged into the swamp blindly on a pretence of bringing water. The Angel walked slowly across the study, sat on the rustic bench, and, through narrowed lids, intently studied the tip of her shoe.

On the trail the Bird Woman wheeled to McLean with a dumbfounded look.

"God!" muttered he.

At last the Bird Woman spoke.

"Do you think the Angel knew she did that?" she asked softly.

"No," said McLean; "I do not. But the poor boy knew it. Heaven help him!"

The Bird Woman stared across the gently waving swale. "I don't see how I am going to blame her," she said at last. "It's so exactly what I would have done myself."

"Say the remainder," demanded McLean, hoarsely. "Do him justice."

"He was born a gentleman," conceded the Bird Woman. "He took no advantage. He never even offered to touch her. Whatever that kiss meant to him, he recognized that it was the loving impulse of a child under stress of strong emotion. He was fine and manly as any man ever could have been."

McLean lifted his hat. "Thank you," he said simply, and parted the bushes for her to enter Freckles' room.

It was her first visit. Before she left she sent for her cameras and made studies of each side of it and of the cathedral. She was entranced with the delicate beauty of the place, while her eyes kept following Freckles as if she could not believe that it could be his conception and work.

That was a happy day. The Bird Woman had brought a lunch, and they spread it, with Freckles' dinner, on the study floor and sat, resting and enjoying themselves. But the Angel put her banjo into its case, silently gathered her music, and no one mentioned the concert.

The Bird Woman left McLean and the Angel to clear away the lunch, and with Freckles examined the walls of his room and told him all she knew about his shrubs and flowers. She analyzed a cardinal-flower and showed him what he had wanted to know all summer—why the bees buzzed ineffectually around it while the humming-birds found in it an ever-ready feast. Some of his specimens were so rare that she was unfamiliar with them, and with the flower-book between them they knelt, studying the different varieties. She wandered the length of the cathedral aisle with him, and it was at her suggestion that he lighted his altar with a row of flaming foxfire.

As Freckles came to the cabin from his long day at the swamp he saw Mrs. Chicken sweeping to the south and wondered where she was going. He stepped into the bright, cosy little kitchen, and as he reached down the wash-basin he asked Mrs. Duncan a question.

"Mother Duncan, do kisses wash off?"

So warm a wave swept her heart that a half-flush mantled her face. She straightened her shoulders and glanced at her hands tenderly.

"Lord, na! Freckles," she cried. "At least, the anes ye get from people ye love dinna. They dinna stay on the outside. They strike in until they find the centre of your heart and make their stopping-place there, and naething can take them from ye—I doubt if even death—— Na, lad, ye can be reet sure kisses dinna wash off!"

Freckles set the basin down and muttered as he plunged his hot, tired face into the water, "I needn't be afraid to be washing, then, for that one struck in."

CHAPTER XI

Wherein the Butterflies Go on a Spree and Freckles Informs the Bird Woman

CHAPTER XI

Wherein the Butterflies Go on a Spree and Freckles Informs the Bird Woman

"I WISH," said Freckles at breakfast one morning, "that I had some way to be sending a message to the Bird Woman. I've something at the swamp that I'm believing never happened before, and surely she'll be wanting it."

"What now, Freckles?" asked Mrs. Duncan.

"Why, the oddest thing you ever heard of," said Freckles; "the whole insect tribe gone on a spree. I'm supposing it's my doings, but it all happened by accident, like. You see, on the swale side of the line, right against me trail, there's one of these scrub wild crabtrees. Where the grass grows thick around it, is the finest place you ever conceived of for snakes. Having women about has set me trying to clean out those fellows a bit, and yesterday I noticed that tree in passing. It struck me that it would be a good idea to be taking it out. First I thought I'd take me hatchet and cut it down, for it ain't thicker than me upper arm. Then I remembered how it was blooming in the spring and filling all the air with sweetness. The colouring of the blossoms is beautiful, and I hated to be killing it. I just cut the grass short all around it. Then I started at the ground, trimmed up the trunk near the height of me shoulder, and left the top spreading. That made it look so truly ornamental that, idle like, I chips off the rough places neat, and this morning, on me soul, it's a sight! You see, cutting off the limbs and trimming up the trunk sets the sap running. In this hot sun it ferments in a few hours. There isn't much room for more things to crowd on that tree than there are, and to get drunker isn't noways possible."

"Weel, I be drawed on!" exclaimed Mrs. Duncan. "What kind of things do ye mean, Freckles?"

"Why, just an army of black ants. Some of them are sucking away like old topers. Some of them are setting up on their tails and hind legs, fiddling with their fore-feet and wiping their eyes. Some are rolling around on the ground, contented. There are quantities of big blue-bottle flies over the bark and hanging on the grasses around, too drunk to steer a course flying; so they just buzz away like flying, and all the time sitting still. The snake-feeders are too full to feed anything—even more sap to themselves. There's a lot of hard-backed bugs—beetles, I guess—coloured like the brown, blue, and black of a peacock's tail. They hang on until the legs of them are so wake they can't stick a minute longer, and then they break away and fall to the ground. They just lay there on their backs, fably clawing air. When it wears off a bit, up they get, and go crawling back for more, and they so full they bump into each other and roll over. Sometimes they can't climb the tree until they wait to sober up a little. There's a lot of big black-and-gold bumble-bees, done for entire, stumbling over the bark and rolling on the ground. They just lay there on their backs, rocking from side to side, singing to themselves like fat, happy babies. The wild bees keep up a steady buzzing with the beating of their wings.

"The butterflies are the worst old topers of them all. They're just a circus! You never saw the like of the beauties! They come every colour you could be naming, and every shape you could be thinking up. They drink and drink until, if I'm driving them away, they stagger as they fly and turn somersaults in the air. If I lave them alone, they cling to the grasses, shivering happy like; and I'm blest, Mother Duncan, if the best of them could be unlocking the front door with a lead-pencil, even."

"I never heard of anything sae surprising," said Mrs. Duncan.

"It's a rare sight to watch them, and no one ever made a picture of a thing like that before, I'm for thinking," said Freckles, earnestly.

"Na," said Mrs. Duncan. "Ye can be pretty sure there didna. The Bird Woman must have word in some way, if ye walk the line and I walk to town and tell her. If ye think ye can wait until after supper, I am most sure ye can gang yoursel', for Duncan is coming home and he'd be glad to watch for ye. If he does na come, and na ane passes that I can send word with to-day, I really will gang early in the morning and tell her mysel'."

Freckles took his lunch and went to the swamp. He walked and watched eagerly. He could find no trace of anything, yet he felt a tense nervousness, as if trouble might be brooding. He examined every section of the wire, and kept watchful eyes on the grasses of the swale, in an effort to discover if any one had passed through them; but he could discover no trace of anything to justify his fears.

He tilted his hat brim to shade his face and looked for his chickens. They were hanging almost beyond sight in the sky.

"Gee!" he said. "If I only had your sharp eyes and convenient location now, I wouldn't need be troubling so."

He reached his room and cautiously scanned the entrance before he stepped in. Then he pushed the bushes apart with his right arm and entered, his left hand on the butt of his favourite revolver. Instantly he knew that some one had been there. He stepped to the centre of the room, closely scanning each wall and the floor. He could find no trace of a clue to confirm his belief, yet so intimate was he with the spirit of the place that he knew.

How he knew he could not have told, yet he did know that some one had entered his room, sat on his benches, and walked over his floor. He was surest around the case. Nothing was disturbed, yet it seemed to Freckles that he could see where prying fingers had tried the lock. He stepped behind the case, carefully examining the ground all around it, and close beside the tree to which it was nailed he found a deep, fresh footprint in the spongy soil—a long, narrow print, that was never made by the foot of Wessner. His heart tugged in his breast as he mentally measured the print, but he did not linger, for now the feeling arose that he was being watched. It seemed to him that he could feel the eyes of some intruder at his back.

He knew he was examining things too closely: if any one were watching, he did not want him to know that he felt it.

He took the most open way, and carried water for his flowers and moss as usual; but he put himself into no position in which he was fully exposed, and his hand was close his revolver constantly. Growing restive at last under the strain, he plunged boldly into the swamp and searched minutely all around his room, but he could not discover the least thing to give him further cause for alarm. He unlocked his case, took out his wheel, and for the remainder of the day he rode and watched as he never had before. Several times he locked the wheel and crossed the swamp on foot, zigzagging to cover all the space possible. Every rod he travelled he used the caution that sprang from knowledge of danger and the direction from which it probably would come. Several times he thought of sending for McLean, but for his life he could not make up his mind to do it with nothing more tangible than one footprint to justify him.

He waited until he was sure Duncan would be at home, if he were coming for the night, before he went to supper. The first thing he saw as he crossed the swale was the big bays in the yard.

There had been no one passing that day, and Duncan readily agreed to watch until Freckles rode to town. He told Duncan of the footprint, and urged him to guard closely. Duncan said he might rest easy, and filling his pipe and taking a good revolver, the big man went to the Limberlost.

Freckles made himself clean and neat, and raced to town, but it was night and the stars were shining before he reached the home of the Bird Woman. From afar he could see that the house was ablaze with lights. The lawn and veranda were strung with fancy lanterns and alive with people. He thought his errand important, so to turn back never occurred to Freckles. This was all the time or opportunity he would have. He must see the Bird Woman, and see her at once. He leaned his wheel inside the fence and walked up the broad front entrance. As he neared the steps, he saw that the place was swarming with young people, and the Angel, with an excuse to a group that surrounded her, came hurrying to him.

"Oh Freckles!" she cried, delightedly. "So you could come? We were so afraid you could not! I'm as glad as I can be!"

"I don't understand," said Freckles. "Were you expecting me?"

"Why of course!" exclaimed the Angel. "Haven't you come to my party? Didn't you get my invitation? I sent you one."

"By mail?" asked Freckles.

"Yes," said the Angel. "I had to help with the preparations, and I couldn't find time to drive out; but I wrote you a letter, and told you that the Bird Woman was giving a party for me, and we wanted you to come, surely. I told them at the office to put it with Mr. Duncan's mail."

"Then that's likely where it is at present," said Freckles. "Duncan comes to town only once a week, and at times not that. He's home to-night for the first in a week. He's watching an hour for me until I come to the Bird Woman with a bit of work I thought she'd be caring to hear about bad. Is she where I can see her?"

The Angel's face clouded.

"What a disappointment!" she cried. "I did so want all my friends to know you. Can't you stay anyway?"

Freckles glanced from his wading-boots to the patent leathers of some of the Angel's friends, and smiled whimsically, but there was no danger of his ever misjudging her again.

"You know I cannot, Angel," he said.

"I am afraid I do," she said ruefully. "It's too bad! But there is a thing I want for you more than to come to my party, and that is to hang on and win with your work. I think of you every day, and I just pray that those thieves are not getting ahead of you. Oh, Freckles, do watch closely!"

She was so lovely a picture as she stood before him, ardent in his cause, that Freckles could not take his eyes from her to notice what her friends were thinking. If she did not mind, why should he? Anyway, if they really were the Angel's friends, probably they were better accustomed to her ways than he.

Her face and bared neck and arms were like the wildrose bloom. Her soft frock of white tulle lifted and stirred around her with the gentle evening air. The beautiful golden hair, that crept around her temples and ears as if it loved to cling there, was caught back and bound with broad blue satin ribbon. There was a sash of blue at her waist, and knots of it catching up her draperies.

"Must I go after the Bird Woman?" she pleaded.

"Indade, you must," answered Freckles, firmly.

The Angel went away, but returned to say that the Bird Woman was telling a story to those inside and she could not come for a short time.

"You won't come in?" she pleaded.

"I must not," said Freckles. "I am not dressed to be among your friends, and I might be forgetting meself and stay too long."

"Then," said the Angel, "we mustn't go through the house, because it would disturb the story; but I want you to come the outside way to the conservatory and have some of my birthday lunch and some cake to take to Mrs. Duncan and the babies. Won't that be fun?"

Freckles thought that it would be more than fun, and followed delightedly.

The Angel gave him a big glass, brimming with some icy, sparkling liquid that struck his palate as it never had been touched before, because a combination of frosty fruit juices had not been a frequent beverage with him. The night was warm, and the Angel most beautiful and kind. A triple delirium of spirit, mind, and body seized upon him and developed a boldness all unnatural. He slightly parted the heavy curtains that separated the conservatory from the company and looked between. He almost stopped breathing. He had read of things like that, but he never had seen them.

The open space seemed to stretch through half a dozen

rooms, all ablaze with lights, perfumed with flowers, and filled with elegantly dressed people. There were glimpses of polished floors, sparkling glass, and fine furnishings. From somewhere, the voice of his beloved Bird Woman arose and fell.

The Angel crowded beside him and was watching also.

"Doesn't it look pretty?" she whispered.

"Do you suppose Heaven is any finer than that?" asked Freckles.

The Angel began to laugh.

"Do you want to be laughing harder than that?" queried Freckles.

"A laugh is always good," said the Angel. "A little more avoirdupois won't hurt me. Go ahead."

"Well then," said Freckles, "it's only that I feel all over as if I belonged there. I could wear fine clothes, and move over those floors, and hold me own against the best of them."

"But where does my laugh come in?" demanded the Angel, as if she had been defrauded.

"And you ask me where the laugh comes in, looking me in the face after that," marvelled Freckles.

"I wouldn't be so foolish as to laugh at such a manifest truth as that," said the Angel. "Any one who knows you even half as well as I do, knows that you are never guilty of a discourtesy, and you move with twice the grace of any man here. Why shouldn't you feel as if you belonged where people are graceful and courteous?"

"On me soul!" said Freckles, "you are kind to be thinking it. You are doubly kind to be saying it."

The curtains parted and a woman came toward them. Her silks and laces trailed across the polished floors. The lights gleamed on her neck and arms, and flashed from rare jewels. She was smiling brightly; and until she spoke, Freckles had not realized fully that it was his loved Bird Woman.

Noticing his bewilderment, she cried: "Why, Freckles! Don't you know me in my war clothes?"

"I do in the uniform in which you fight the Limberlost," said Freckles.

The Bird Woman laughed. Then he told her why he had come, but she scarcely could believe him. She could not say exactly when she would go, but she would make it as soon as possible, for she was most anxious for the study.

While they talked, the Angel was busy packing a box of sandwiches, cake, fruit, and flowers. She gave him a last frosty glass, thanked him repeatedly for bringing news of new material; then Freckles went into the night. He rode toward the Limberlost with his eyes on the stars. Presently he removed his hat, hung it to his belt, and ruffled his hair to the sweep of the night wind. He filled the air all the way with snatches of oratorios, gospel hymns, and dialect and coon songs, in a startlingly varied programme. The one thing Freckles knew that he could do was to sing. The Duncans heard him coming a mile up the corduroy and could not believe their senses. Freckles unfastened the box from his belt, and gave Mrs. Duncan and the children all the eatables it contained, except one big piece of cake that he carried to the sweet-loving Duncan. He put the flowers back in the box and set it among his books.

He did not say anything, but they understood it was not to be touched.

"Thae's Freckles' flow'rs," said a tiny Scotsman, "but," he added cheerfully, "it's oor sweeties!"

Freckles' face slowly flushed as he took Duncan's cake and started toward the swamp. While Duncan ate, Freckles told him something about the evening, as well as he could find words to express himself, and the big man was so amazed he kept forgetting the treat in his hands.

Then Freckles mounted his wheel and began a spin that terminated only when the biggest Plymouth Rock in Duncan's coop saluted a new day, and long lines of light reddened the east. As he rode he sang, while he sang he worshipped, but the god he tried to glorify was a dim and far-away mystery. The Angel was warm flesh and blood.

Every time he passed the little bark-covered imprint on the trail he dismounted, removed his hat, solemnly knelt and laid his lips on the impression. Because he kept no account himself, only the laughing-faced old man of the moon knew how often it happened; and as from the beginning, to the follies of earth that gentleman has ever been kind.

With the near approach of dawn Freckles tuned his last note. Wearied almost to falling, he turned from the trail into the path leading to the cabin for a few hours' rest.

CHAPTER XII

Wherein Black Jack Captures Freckles and the Angel Captures Jack

CHAPTER XII

Wherein Black Jack Captures Freckles and the Angel Captures Jack

As FRECKLES left the trail, from the swale close the south entrance, four large muscular men arose and swiftly and carefully entered the swamp by the wagon-road. Two of them carried a big saw, the third, coils of rope and wire, and all of them were heavily armed. They left one man on guard at the entrance. The other three made their way through the darkness as best they could, and were soon at Freckles' room. He had left the swamp on his wheel from the west trail. They counted on his returning on the wheel and circling the east line before he came there.

A little below the west entrance to Freckles' room, Black Jack stepped into the swale, and binding a wire tightly around a scrub oak, carried it below the waving grasses, stretched it taut across the trail, and fastened it to a tree in the swamp. Then he obliterated all signs of his work, and arranged the grass over the wire until it was so completely covered that only minute examination would reveal it. They entered Freckles' room with coarse oaths and jests. In a few moments, his specimen case with its precious contents was rolled into the swamp, while the saw was eating into one of the finest trees of the Limberlost.

The first report from the man on watch was that Duncan had driven to the South camp; the second, that Freckles was coming. The man watching was sent to see on which side the boy turned into the path; as they had expected, he took the east. He was a little tired and his head was rather stupid, for he had not been able to sleep as he had hoped, but he was very happy. Although he watched until his eyes ached, he could see no sign of any one having entered the swamp.

He called a cheery greeting to all his chickens. At Sleepy Snake Creek he almost fell from his wheel with surprise: the saw-bird was surrounded by four lanky youngsters clamouring for breakfast. The father was strutting with all the importance of a drum-major.

"No use to expect the Bird Woman to-day," said Freckles; "but now wouldn't she be jumping for a chance at that?"

As soon as Freckles was far down the east line, the watch was posted below the room on the west to report his coming. It was only a few moments before the signal came. Then the saw stopped, and the rope was brought out and uncoiled close to a sapling. Wessner and Black Jack crowded to the very edge of the swamp a little above the wire, and crouched, waiting.

They heard Freckles before they saw him. He came gliding down the line swiftly, and as he rode he was singing softly:

> "Oh, do you love,
> Oh, say you love——"

He got no farther. The sharply driven wheel struck the

tense wire and bounded back. Freckles shot over the handlebar and coasted down the trail on his chest. As he struck, Black Jack and Wessner were upon him. Wessner caught off an old felt hat and clapped it over Freckles' mouth, while Black Jack twisted the boy's arms behind him and they rushed him into his room. Almost before he realized that anything had happened, he was trussed to a tree and securely gagged.

Then three of the men resumed work on the tree. The other followed the path Freckles had worn to Little Chicken's tree, and presently he reported that the wires were down and two teams with the loading apparatus coming to take out the timber. All the time the saw was slowly eating, eating into the big tree.

Wessner went to the trail and removed the wire. He picked up Freckles' wheel, that did not seem to be injured, and leaned it against the bushes so that if any one did pass on the trail he would not see it doubled in the swamp-grass.

Then he came and stood in front of Freckles and laughed in devilish hate. To his own amazement, Freckles found himself looking fear in the face, and marvelled that he was not afraid. Four to one! The tree half-way eaten through, the wagons coming up the inside road—he, bound and gagged! The men with Black Jack and Wessner had belonged to McLean's gang when last he had heard of them, but who those coming with the wagons might be he could not guess.

If they secured that tree, McLean lost its value, lost his wager, and lost his faith in him. The words of the Angel hammered in his ears. "Oh, Freckles, do watch closely!"

The saw worked steadily.

When the tree was down and loaded, what would they do? Pull out, and leave him there to report them? It was not to be hoped for. The place always had been lawless. It could mean but one thing.

A mist swept before his eyes, while his head swam. Was it only last night that he had worshipped the Angel in a delirium of happiness? And now, what? Wessner, released from a turn at the saw, walked to the flower-bed, and tearing up a handful of rare ferns by the roots, started toward Freckles. His intention was obvious. Black Jack stopped him, with an oath.

"You see here, Dutchy," he bawled, "mebby you think you'll wash his face with that, but you won't. A contract's a contract. We agreed to take out these trees and leave him for you to dispose of whatever way you please, provided you shut him up eternally on this deal. But I'll not see a tied man tormented by a fellow that he can lick up the ground with, loose, and that's flat. It raises my gorge to think what he'll get when we're gone, but you needn't think you're free to begin before. Don't you lay a hand on him while I'm here! What do you say, boys?"

"I say yes," growled one of McLean's latest deserters. "What's more, we're a pack of fools to risk the dirty work of silencing him. You had him face down and you on his back; why the hell didn't you cover his head and roll him into the bushes until we were gone? When I went into this, I didn't understand that he was to see all of us and that there was murder on the ticket. I'm not up to it. I don't mind lifting trees we came for, but I'm cursed if I want blood on my hands."

"Well, you ain't going to get it," bellowed Jack. "You fellows only contracted to help me get out my marked trees. He belongs to Wessner, and it ain't in our deal what happens to him."

"Yes, and if Wessner finishes him safely, we are practically in for murder as well as stealing the trees; and if he don't, all hell's to pay. I think you've made a damnable bungle of this thing; that's what I think!"

"Then keep your thoughts to yourself," cried Jack. "We're doing this, and it's all planned safe and sure. As for killing that buck—come to think of it, killing is what he needs. He's away too good for this world of woe, anyhow. I tell you, it's all safe enough. His dropping out won't be the only secret the old Limberlost has never told. It's too dead easy to make it look like he helped take the timber and then cut. Why, he's played right into our hands. He was here at the swamp all last night, and back again in an hour or so. When we get our plan worked out, even old fool Duncan won't lift a finger to look for his carcass. We couldn't have him going in better shape."

"You just bet," said Wessner. "I owe him all he'll get, and be damned to you, but I'll pay!" he snarled at Freckles.

So it was killing, then. They were not only after this one tree, but many, and with his body it was their plan to kill his honour. To brand him a thief, with them, before the Angel, the Bird Woman, the dear Boss, and the Duncans—Freckles, in sick despair, sagged against the ropes.

Then he gathered his forces and thought swiftly. There was no hope of McLean's coming. They had chosen a day when they knew he had a big contract at the South camp. The Boss could not come before to-morrow by any possibility, and there would be no to-morrow for the boy. Duncan was on his way to the South camp, and the Bird Woman had said she would come as soon as she could. After the fatigue of the party, it was useless to expect her and the Angel to-day, and God save them from coming! The Angel's father had said they would be as safe in the Limberlost as at home. What would he think of this?

The sweat broke on Freckles' forehead. He tugged at the ropes whenever he felt that he dared, but they were passed around the tree and his body several times, and knotted on his chest. He was helpless. There was no hope, no help. And after they had conspired to make him appear a runaway thief to his loved ones, what was it that Wessner would do to him?

Whatever it was, Freckles lifted his head and resolved that he would bear in mind what he had once heard the Bird Woman say. He would go out bonnily. Never would he let them see, if he grew afraid. After all, what did it matter what they did to his body if by some scheme of the devil they could encompass his disgrace?

Then hope suddenly rose high in Freckles' breast. They could not do that! The Angel would not believe. Neither would McLean. He would keep up his courage. Kill him they could; dishonour him they could not.

Yet, summon all the fortitude he might, that saw eating into the tree rasped his nerves worse and worse. With whirling brain he gazed into the Limberlost, searching for something, he knew not what, and in blank horror found his eyes focussing on the Angel. She was quite a distance away, but he could see her white lips and angry expression.

Last week he had taken her and the Bird Woman across the swamp over the path he followed in going from his room to the chicken tree. He had told them the night before, that the butterfly tree was on the line close to this path. In figuring on their not coming that day, he failed to reckon with the enthusiasm of the Bird Woman. They must be there for the study, and the Angel had risked crossing the swamp in search of him. Or was there something in his room they needed? The blood surged in his ears as the roar of the Limberlost in the wrath of a storm.

He looked again, and it had been a dream. She was not there. Had she been? For his life, Freckles could not tell whether he really had seen the Angel, or whether his strained senses had played him the most cruel trick of all. Or was it not the kindest? Now he could go with the vision of her lovely face fresh with him.

"Thank You for that, oh God!" whispered Freckles. "'Twas more than kind of You and I don't s'pose I ought to be wanting anything else; but if You can, oh, I wish I could know before this ends, if 'twas me mother"—Freckles could not even whisper the words, for he hesitated a second and ended—"*if 'twas me mother did it!*"

"Freckles! Freckles! Oh, Freckles!" the voice of the Angel came calling. Freckles swayed forward and wrenched at the rope until it cut deeply into his body.

"Hell!" cried Black Jack. "Who is that? Do you know?"

Freckles nodded.

Jack whipped out a revolver and snatched the gag from Freckles' mouth.

"Say quick, or it's up with you right now, and whoever that is with you!"

"It's the girl the Bird Woman takes with her," whispered Freckles through dry, swollen lips.

"They ain't due here for five days yet," said Wessner. "We got on to that last week."

"Yes," said Freckles; "but I found a tree covered with butterflies and things along the east line yesterday that I thought the Bird Woman would want extra, and I went to town to tell her last night. She said she'd come soon, but she didn't say when. They must be here. I take care of the girl while the Bird Woman works. Untie me quick until she is gone. I'll try to send her back, and then you can go on with your dirty work."

"He ain't lying," volunteered Wessner. "I saw that tree covered with butterflies and him watching around it when we were spying on him yesterday."

"No, he leaves lying to your sort," snapped Black Jack, as he undid the rope and pitched it across the room. "Remember that you're covered every move you make, my buck," he cautioned.

"Freckles! Freckles!" came the Angel's impatient voice, closer and closer.

"I must be answering," said Freckles, and Jack nodded. "Right here!" he called, and to the men: "You go on with your work, and remember one thing yourselves. The work of the Bird Woman is known all over the world. This girl's father is a rich man, and she is all he has. If you offer hurt of any kind to either of them, this world has no place far enough away or dark enough for you to be hiding in. Hell will be easy to what any man will get if he touches either of them!"

"Freckles, where are you?" demanded the Angel.

Soulsick with fear for her, Freckles went toward her and parted the bushes that she might enter. She came through without apparently giving him a glance, and the first words she said were: "Why have the gang come so soon? I didn't know you expected them for three weeks yet. Or is this some especial tree that Mr. McLean needs to fill an order right now?"

Freckles hesitated. Would a man dare lie to save himself? No. But to save the Angel—surely that was different. He opened his lips, but the Angel was capable of saving herself. She walked among them, exactly as if she had been reared in a lumber-camp, and never waited for an answer.

"Why, your specimen case!" she cried. "Look! Haven't you noticed that it's tipped over? Set it straight, quickly!"

A couple of the men stepped out and carefully righted the case.

"There! That's better," she said. "Freckles, I'm surprised at your being so careless. It would be a shame to break those lovely butterflies for one old tree! Is that a valuable tree? Why didn't you tell us last night you were going to take out a tree this morning? Oh, say, did you put your case there to protect that tree from that stealing old Black Jack and his gang? I bet you did! Well, if that wasn't bright! What kind of a tree is it?"

"It's a white oak," said Freckles.

"Like those they make dining-tables and sideboards from?"

"Yes."

"My! How interesting!" she cried. "I don't know a thing about timber, but my father wants me to learn just everything I can. I am going to ask him to let me come here and watch you until I know enough to boss a gang myself. Do you like to cut trees, gentlemen?" she asked with angelic sweetness of the men.

Some of them appeared foolish and some grim, but one managed to say they did.

Then the Angel's eyes turned full on Black Jack, and she gave the most natural little start of astonishment.

"Oh! I almost thought that you were a ghost!" she cried. "But I see now that you are really and truly. Were you ever in Colorado?"

"No," said Jack.

"I see you aren't the same man," said the Angel. "You know, we were in Colorado last year, and there was a cowboy who was the handsomest man anywhere around. He'd come riding into town every night, and all we girls just adored him! Oh, but he was a beauty! I thought at first glance you were really he, but I see now he wasn't nearly so tall nor so broad as you, and only half as handsome."

The men began to laugh while Jack flushed crimson. The Angel joined in the laugh.

"Well, I'll leave it to you! Isn't he handsome?" she challenged. "As for that cowboy's face, it couldn't be compared with yours. The only trouble with you is that your clothes are spoiling you. It's the dress those cowboys wear that makes half their attraction. If you were properly clothed, you could break the heart of the prettiest girl in the country."

With one accord the other men looked at Black Jack, and for the first time realized that he was a superb specimen of manhood, for he stood six feet tall, was broad, well-rounded, and had dark, even skin, big black eyes, and full red lips.

"I'll tell you what!" exclaimed the Angel. "I'd just love to see you on horseback. Nothing sets a handsome man off so splendidly. Do you ride?"

"Yes," said Jack, and his eyes were burning on the Angel as if he would fathom the depths of her soul.

"Well," said the Angel winsomely, "I know what I just wish you'd do. I wish you would let your hair grow a little longer. Then wear a blue flannel shirt a little open at the throat, a red tie, and a broad-brimmed felt hat, and ride past my house of evenings. I'm always at home then, and almost always on the veranda, and, oh! but I would like to see you! Will you do that for me?"

It is impossible to describe the art with which the Angel asked the question. She was looking straight into Jack's face, coarse and hardened with sin and careless living, which was now taking on a wholly different expression.

The evil lines of it were softening and fading under her clear gaze. A dull red flamed into his bronze cheeks, while his eyes were growing brightly tender.

"Yes," he said, and the glance he gave the men was of such a nature that no one saw fit even to change countenance.

"Oh, goody!" she cried, tilting on her toes. "I'll ask all the girls to come see, but they needn't stick in! We can get along without them, can't we?"

Jack leaned toward her. He was the charmed fluttering bird, while the Angel was the snake.

"Well, I rather guess!" he cried.

The Angel drew a deep breath and surveyed him rapturously.

"My, but you're tall!" she commented. "Do you suppose I ever will grow to reach your shoulders?"

She stood on tip toe and measured the distance with her eyes. Then she developed timid confusion, while her glance sought the ground.

"I wish I could do something," she half whispered.

Jack seemed to increase an inch in height.

"What?" he asked hoarsely.

"Lariat Bill used always to have a bunch of red flowers in his shirt pocket. The red lit up his dark eyes and olive cheeks and made him splendid. May I put some red flowers on you?"

Freckles stared as he wheezed for breath. He wished the earth would open and swallow him. Was he dead or alive? Since his Angel had seen Black Jack she never had glanced his way. Was she completely bewitched?

Would she throw herself at the man's feet before them all? Couldn't she give him even one thought? Hadn't she seen that he was gagged and bound? Did she truly think that these were McLean's men? Why, she could not! It was only a few days ago that she had been close enough to this man and angry enough with him to peel the hat from his head with a shot! Suddenly a thing she had said jestingly to him one day came back with startling force: "You must take Angels on trust." Of course you must! She was his Angel. She must have seen! His life, and what was far more, her own, was in her hands. There was nothing he could do but trust her. Surely she was working out some plan.

The Angel knelt beside his flower-bed and recklessly tore up by the roots a big bunch of foxfire.

"These stems are so tough and sticky," she said. "I can't break them. Loan me your knife," she ordered Freckles.

As she reached for the knife, her back was for one second toward the men. She looked into his eyes and deliberately winked.

She severed the stems, tossed the knife to Freckles, and walking to Jack, laid the flowers over his heart.

Freckles broke into a sweat of agony. He had said she would be safe in a herd of howling savages. Would she? If Black Jack even made a motion toward touching her, Freckles knew that from somewhere he would muster the strength to kill him. He mentally measured the distance to where his club lay and set his muscles for a spring. But no—by the splendour of God! The big fellow was baring his head with a hand that was unsteady. The Angel pulled one of the long silver pins from her hat and fastened her flowers securely.

Freckles was quaking. What was to come next? What was she planning, and oh! did she understand the danger of her presence among those men; the real necessity for action?

As the Angel stepped from Jack, she turned her head to one side and peered at him, quite as Freckles had seen the little yellow fellow do on the line a hundred times, and said: "Well, that does the trick! Isn't that fine? See how it sets him off, boys? Don't you forget the tie is to be red, and the first ride soon. I can't wait very long. Now I must go. The Bird Woman will be ready to start, and she will come here hunting me next, for she is busy to-day. What did I come here for anyway?"

She glanced inquiringly around, and several of the men laughed. Oh, the delight of it! She had forgotten her errand for him! Jack had a second increase in height. The Angel glanced helplessly as if seeking a clue. Then her eyes fell, as if by accident, on Freckles, and she cried, "Oh, I know now! It was those magazines the Bird Woman promised you. I came to tell you that we put them under the box where we hide things, at the entrance to the swamp as we came in. I knew I would need my hands crossing the swamp, so I hid them there. You'll find them at the same old place."

Then Freckles spoke.

"It's mighty risky for you to be crossing the swamp alone," he said. "I'm surprised that the Bird Woman would be letting you try it. I know it's a little farther, but it's begging you I am to be going back by the trail. That's bad enough, but it's far safer than the swamp."

The Angel laughed merrily.

"Oh stop your nonsense!" she cried. "I'm not afraid! Not in the least! The Bird Woman didn't want me to try following a path that I'd been over only once, but I was sure I could do it, and I'm rather proud of the performance. Now, don't go babying! You know I'm not afraid!"

"No," said Freckles gently, "I know you're not; but that has nothing to do with the fact that your friends are afraid for you. On the trail you can see your way a bit ahead, and you've all the world a better chance if you meet a snake."

Then Freckles had an inspiration. He turned to Jack imploringly.

"You tell her!" he pleaded. "Tell her to go by the trail. She will for you."

The implication of this statement was so gratifying to Black Jack that he seemed again to expand and take on increase before their very eyes.

"You bet!" exclaimed Jack. And to the Angel: "You better take Freckles' word for it, Miss. He knows the old swamp better than any of us, except me, and if he says 'go by the trail,' you'd best do it."

The Angel hesitated. She wanted to recross the swamp and try to reach the horse. She knew Freckles would brave any danger to save her crossing the swamp alone, but she really was not afraid, while the trail added over a mile to the walk. She knew the path. She intended to run for dear life the instant she felt herself from their sight, and tucked in the folds of her blouse was a fine little 32-calibre revolver that her father had presented her for her share in what he was pleased to call her military exploit. One last glance at Freckles showed her the agony in his eyes, and immediately she imagined he had some other reason. She would follow the trail.

"All right," she said, giving Jack a thrilling glance. "If you say so, I'll return by the trail to please you. Good-bye, everybody."

She lifted the bushes and started toward the entrance.

"You damned fool! Stop her!" growled Wessner. "Keep her till we're loaded, anyhow. You're playing hell! Can't you see that when this thing is found out, there she'll be to ruin all of us. If you let her go, every man of us has got to cut, and some of us will be caught sure."

Jack sprang forward. Freckles' heart muffled in his throat. The Angel seemed to divine Jack's coming. She was humming a little song. She deliberately stopped and began pulling the heads of the curious grasses that grew all around her. When she straightened, she took a step backward and called: "Ho! Freckles, the Bird Woman wants that natural history pamphlet returned. It belongs to a set she is going to have bound. That's one of the reasons we put it under the box. You be sure to get them as you go home to-night, for fear it rains or becomes damp with the heavy dews."

"All right," said Freckles, but it was in a voice that he never had heard before.

Then the Angel turned and sent a parting glance at Jack. She was overpoweringly human and bewitchingly lovely.

"You won't forget that ride and the red tie," she half asserted, half questioned.

Jack succumbed. Freckles was his captive, but he was the Angel's, soul and body. His face wore the holiest look it ever had known as he softly re-echoed Freckles': "All right." With her head held well up, the Angel walked slowly away, and Jack turned to the men.

"Drop your damned staring and saw wood," he shouted. "Don't you know anything at all about how to treat a lady?"

It might have been a question which of the crones that crouched over green wood fires in the cabins of Wildcat Hollow, eternally sucking a corncob pipe and stirring the endless kettles of stewing coon and opossum, had taught him to do even as well as he had by the Angel.

The men muttered and threatened among themselves, but they began working desperately. Some one suggested that a man be sent to follow the Angel and to watch her and the Bird Woman leave the swamp. Freckles' heart sank within him, but Jack was in a delirium and past all caution.

"Yes," he sneered. "Mebby all of you had better give over on the saw and run after the girl. I guess not! Seems to me I got the favours. I didn't see no bouquets on the rest of you! If anybody follows her, I do, and I'm needed here among such a pack of idiots. There's no danger in that baby face. She wouldn't give me away! You double and work like forty, while me and Wessner will take the axes and begin to cut in on the other side."

"What about the noise?" asked Wessner.

"No difference about the noise," answered Jack. "She took us to be from McLean's gang, slick as grease. Make the chips fly!"

So all of them attacked the big tree.

Freckles sat on one of his benches and waited. In their haste to fell the tree and load it, so that the teamsters could start, and leave them free to attack another, they had forgotten to rebind him.

The Angel was on the trail and safely started. The cold perspiration made Freckles' temples clammy and ran in little streams down his chest. It would take her more time to follow the trail, but her safety was Freckles' sole thought in urging her to go that way. He tried to figure on how long it would require to walk to the carriage. He wondered if the Bird Woman had unhitched. He followed the Angel every step of the way. He figured on when she would cross the path of the clearing, pass the deep pool where his "find-out" frog lived, cross Sleepy Snake Creek, and reach the carriage.

He wondered what she would say to the Bird Woman, and how long it would take them to pack and start. He knew now that they would understand, and the Angel would try to get the Boss there in time to save his wager. She could never do it, for the saw was over half through, and Jack and Wessner cutting into the opposite side of the tree. It appeared as if they could fell at least that tree, before McLean could come, and if they did he lost his wager.

When it was down, would they rebind him and leave him for Wessner to wreak his insane vengeance on, or would they take him along to the next tree and dispose of him when they had stolen all the timber they could? Jack had said that he should not be touched until he left. Surely he would not run all that risk for one tree, when he had many others of far greater value marked. Freckles felt that he had some hope to cling to now, but he found himself praying that the Angel would hurry.

Once Jack came to Freckles and asked if he had any water. Freckles arose and showed him where he kept his drinking water. Jack drank in great gulps, and as he passed back the bucket, he said: "When a man's got a chance of catching a fine girl like that, he ought not be mixed up in any dirty business. I wish to God I was out of this!"

Freckles answered heartily: "I wish I was, too!"

Jack stared at him a minute and then broke into a roar of rough laughter.

"Blest if I blame you," he said. "But you had your chance! We offered you a fair thing and you gave Wessner his answer. I ain't envying you when he gives you his."

"You're six to one," answered Freckles. "It will be easy enough for you to be killing the body of me, but, curse you all, you can't blacken me soul!"

"Well, I'd give anything you could name if I had your honesty," said Jack.

When the mighty tree fell, the Limberlost shivered and screamed with the echo. Freckles groaned in despair, but the gang took heart. That was so much accomplished.

They knew where to dispose of it safely, with no questions asked. Before the day was over, they could remove three others, all suitable for veneer and worth far more than this. Then they would leave Freckles to Wessner and scatter for safety, with more money than they had ever hoped for in their possession.

CHAPTER XIII

Wherein the Angel Releases Freckles, and the Curse of Black Jack Falls upon Her

CHAPTER XIII

Wherein the Angel Releases Freckles, and the Curse of Black Jack Falls upon Her

ON THE line, the Angel gave one backward glance at Black Jack, to see that he had returned to his work. Then she gathered her skirts above her knees and leaped forward on the run. In the first three yards she passed Freckles' wheel. Instantly she imagined that was why he had insisted on her coming by the trail. She seized it and sprang on. The saddle was too high, but she was an expert rider and could catch the pedals as they came up. She stopped at Duncan's cabin long enough to remedy this, telling Mrs. Duncan while working what was happening, and for her to follow the east trail until she found the Bird Woman, and told her that she had gone after McLean and for her to leave the swamp as quickly as possible.

Even with her fear for Freckles to spur her, Sarah Duncan blanched and began shivering at the idea of facing the Limberlost. The Angel looked her in the eyes.

"No matter how afraid you are, you have to go," she said. "If you don't the Bird Woman will go to Freckles' room, hunting me, and they will have trouble with her. If she isn't told to leave at once, they may follow me, and, finding I'm gone, do some terrible thing to Freckles. I can't go—that's flat—for if they caught me, then there'd be no one to go for help. You don't suppose they are going to take out the trees they're after and then leave Freckles to run and tell? They are going to murder the boy; that's what they are going to do. You run, and run for life! For Freckles' life! You can ride back with the Bird Woman."

The Angel saw Mrs. Duncan started; then began her race.

Those awful miles of corduroy! Would they never end? She did not dare use the wheel too roughly, for if it broke she never could arrive on time afoot. Where her way was impassable for the wheel, she jumped off, and pushing it beside her or carrying it, she ran as fast as she could. The day was fearfully warm. The sun poured with the fierce baking heat of August. The bushes claimed her hat, and she did not stop for it.

Where it was at all possible, the Angel mounted and pounded over the corduroy again. She was panting for breath and almost worn out when she reached the level pike. She had no idea how long she had been—and only two miles covered. She leaned over the bars, almost standing on the pedals, racing with all the strength in her body. The blood surged in her ears while her head swam, but she kept a straight course, and rode and rode. It seemed to her that she was standing still, while the trees and houses were racing past her.

Once a farmer's big dog rushed angrily into the road and she swerved until she almost fell, but she regained her balance, and setting her muscles, pedalled as fast as she could. At last she lifted her head. Surely it could not be over a mile more. She had covered two of corduroy and at least three of gravel, and it was only six in all.

She was reeling in the saddle, but she gripped the bars with new energy, and raced desperately. The sun beat on her bare head and hands. Just when she was choking with dust, and almost prostrate with heat and exhaustion—crash, she ran into a broken bottle. Snap! went the tire; the wheel swerved and pitched over. The Angel rolled into the thick yellow dust of the road and lay quietly.

From afar, Duncan began to notice a strange, dust-covered object in the road, as he headed toward town with the first load of the day's felling.

He chirruped to the bays and hurried them all he could. As he neared the Angel, he saw it was a woman and a broken wheel. He was beside her in an instant. He carried her to a shaded fence-corner, stretched her on the grass, and wiped the dust from the lovely face all dirt-streaked, crimson, and bearing a startling whiteness around the mouth and nose.

Wheels were common enough. Many of the farmers' daughters owned and rode them, but he knew these same farmers' daughters; this face was a stranger's. He glanced at the Angel's tumbled clothing, the silkiness of her hair, with its pale satin ribbon, and noticed that she had lost her hat. Her lips tightened in an ominous quiver. He left her and picked up the wheel: as he had surmised, he knew it. This, then, was Freckles' Swamp Angel. There was trouble in the Limberlost, and she had broken down racing to McLean. Duncan turned the bays into a fence-corner, tied one of them, unharnessed the other, fastened up the trace chains, and hurried to the nearest farmhouse to send help to the Angel. He found a woman, who took a bottle of camphor, a jug of water, and some towels, and started on the run.

Then Duncan put the bay to speed and raced to camp.

The Angel, left alone, lay still for a second, then she shivered and opened her eyes. She saw that she was on the grass and the broken wheel beside her. Instantly she realized that some one had carried her there and gone after help. She sat up and looked around. She noticed the load of logs and the one horse. Some one was riding after help for her!

"Oh, poor Freckles!" she wailed. "They may be killing him by now. Oh, how much time have I wasted?"

She hurried to the other bay, her fingers flying as she set him free. Snatching up a big blacksnake whip that laid on the ground, she caught the hames, stretched along the horse's neck, and, for the first time, the fine, big fellow felt on his back the quality of the lash that Duncan was accustomed to crack over him. He was frightened, and ran at top speed.

The Angel passed a wildly waving, screaming woman on the road, and a little later a man riding as if he, too, were in great haste. The man called to her, but she only lay lower and used the whip. Soon the feet of the man's horse sounded farther and farther away.

At the South camp they were loading a second wagon, when the Angel appeared riding one of Duncan's bays, lathered and dripping, and cried: "Everybody go to

Freckles! There are thieves stealing trees, and they had him bound. They're going to kill him!"

She wheeled the horse toward the Limberlost. The alarm sounded through camp. The gang were not unprepared. McLean sprang to Nellie's back and raced after the Angel. As they passed Duncan, he wheeled and followed. Soon the pike was an irregular procession of barebacked riders, wildly driving flying horses toward the swamp.

The Boss rode neck-and-neck with the Angel. He repeatedly commanded her to stop and fall out of line, until he remembered that he would need her to lead him to Freckles. Then he gave up and rode beside her, for she was sending the bay at as sharp a pace as the other horses could keep and hold out. He could see that she was not hearing him. He glanced back and saw that Duncan was close. There was something terrifying in the appearance of the big man, and the manner in which he sat his beast and rode. It would be a sad day for the man on whom Duncan's wrath broke. There were four others close behind him, and the pike filling with the remainder of the gang; so McLean took heart and raced beside the Angel. Over and over he asked her where the trouble was, but she only gripped the hames, leaned along the bay's neck, and slashed away with the blacksnake. The steaming horse, with crimson nostrils and heaving sides, stretched out and ran for home with all the speed there was in him.

When they passed the cabin, the Bird Woman's carriage was there and Mrs. Duncan in the door wringing her hands, but the Bird Woman was nowhere to be seen. The Angel sent the bay along the path and turned into the west trail, while the men bunched and followed her. When she reached the entrance to Freckles' room, there were four men with her, and two more very close behind. She slid from the horse, and snatching the little revolver from her pocket, darted toward the bushes. McLean caught them back, and with drawn weapon, pressed beside her. There they stopped in astonishment.

The Bird Woman blocked the entrance. Over a small limb lay her revolver. It was trained at short range on Black Jack and Wessner, who stood with their hands above their heads.

Freckles, with the blood trickling down his face, from an ugly cut in his temple, was gagged and bound to the tree again; the remainder of the men were gone. Black Jack was raving as a maniac, and when they looked closer it was only the left arm that he raised. His right, with the hand shattered, hung helpless at his side, while his revolver laid at Freckles' feet. Wessner's weapon was in his belt, and beside him Freckles' club.

Freckles' face was white, with colourless lips, but in his eyes was the strength of undying courage. McLean pushed past the Bird Woman crying: "Hold steady on them only one minute more!"

He snatched the revolver from Wessner's belt, and stooped for Jack's.

At that instant the Angel rushed past. She tore the gag from Freckles, and seizing the rope knotted on his chest, she tugged at it desperately. Under her fingers it gave way, and she hurled it to McLean. The men were crowding in, and Duncan seized Wessner. As the Angel saw Freckles stand out, free, she reached her arms to him and pitched forward. A fearful oath burst from the lips of Black Jack. To have saved his life, Freckles could not have avoided the glance of triumph he gave Jack, when folding the Angel in his arms and stretching her on the mosses.

The Bird Woman cried out sharply for water as she ran to them. Some one sprang to bring that, and another to break open the case for brandy. As McLean arose from binding Wessner, there was a cry that Jack was escaping.

He was already far in the swamp, running for its densest part in leaping bounds. Every man who could be spared plunged after him.

Other members of the gang arriving, were sent to follow the tracks of the wagons. The teamsters had driven from the west entrance, and crossing the swale, had taken the same route the Bird Woman and the Angel had before them. There had been ample time for the drivers to reach the road; after that they could take any one of four directions. Traffic was heavy, and lumber-wagons were passing almost constantly, so the men turned back and joined the more exciting hunt for a man. The remainder of the gang joined them, also farmers of the region and travellers attracted by the disturbance.

Watchers were set along the trail at short intervals. They patrolled the line and roads through the swamp that night, with lighted torches, and the next day McLean headed as thorough a search as he felt could be made of one side, while Duncan covered the other; but Black Jack could not be found. Spies were set around his home, in Wildcat Hollow, to ascertain if he reached there or aid was being sent in any direction to him; but it was soon clear that his relatives were ignorant of his hiding-place, and were searching for him.

Great is the elasticity of youth. A hot bath and a sound night's sleep renewed Freckles' strength, and it needed but little more to work the same result with the Angel. Freckles was on the trail early the next morning. Besides a crowd of people anxious to witness Jack's capture, he found four stalwart guards, one at each turn. In his heart he was compelled to admit that he was glad to have them there. Close noon, McLean placed his men in charge of Duncan, and taking Freckles, drove to town to see how the Angel fared. McLean visited a greenhouse and bought an armload of its finest products; but Freckles would have none of them. He would carry his message in a glowing mass of the Limberlost's first golden-rod.

The Bird Woman received them, and in answer to their eager inquiries, said that the Angel was in no way seriously injured, only so bruised and shaken that their doctor had ordered her to lie quietly for the day. Though she was sore and stiff, they were having work to keep her in bed. Her callers sent up their flowers with their grateful regards, and the Angel promptly returned word that she wanted to see them.

She reached both hands to McLean. "What if one old tree is gone? You don't care, sir? You feel that Freckles has kept his trust as nobody ever did before, don't you? You won't forget all those long first days of fright that you told us of, the fearful cold of winter, the rain, heat, and lonesomeness, and the brave days, and lately, nights, too, and let him feel that his trust is broken? Oh, Mr. McLean," she begged, "say something to him! Do something to make him feel that it isn't for nothing he has watched and suffered it out with that old Limberlost. Make him see how great and fine it is, and how far, far better he has done than you or any of us expected! What's one old tree, anyway?" she cried passionately.

"I was thinking before you came. Those other men were rank big cowards. They were scared for their lives. If they were the drivers, I wager you gloves against gloves they never took those logs out to the pike. My coming upset them. Before you feel bad any more, you go look and see if they didn't lose courage the minute they left Wessner and Black Jack, dump that timber and run. I don't believe they ever had the grit to drive out with it in daylight. Go see if they didn't figure on leaving the way we did the other morning, and you'll find the logs before you reach the road. They never risked taking them into the open, when they got away and had time to think. Of course they didn't!

"And, then, another thing. You haven't lost your wager! It never will be claimed, because you made it with a stout, dark, red-faced man who drives a bay and a gray. He was right back of you, Mr. McLean, when I came yesterday. He went deathly white and shook on his feet when he saw those men probably would be caught. Some one of them was something to him, and you can just spot him for one of the men at the bottom of your troubles, and urging those younger fellows to steal from you. I suppose he'd promised to divide. You settle with him, and that business will stop."

She turned to Freckles. "And you be the happiest man alive, because you have kept your trust. Go look where I tell you and you'll find the logs. I can see just about where they are. When they go up that steep little hill, into the next woods after the corn-field, why, they could unloose the chains and the logs would roll from the wagons themselves. Now, you go look; and Mr. McLean, you do feel that Freckles has been brave and faithful? You won't love him any the less even if you don't find the logs——"

The Angel's nerve gave way and she began to cry. Freckles could not endure it. He almost ran from the room, with the tears in his eyes; but McLean took the Angel from the Bird Woman's arms, and kissed her brave little face, stroked her hair, and petted her into quietness before he left.

As they drove to the swamp, McLean so earnestly seconded all that the Angel had said that he soon had the boy feeling much better.

"Freckles, your Angel has a spice of the devil in her, but she's superb! You needn't spend any time questioning or bewailing anything she does. Just worship blindly, my boy. By heaven! she's sense, courage, and beauty for half a dozen girls," said McLean.

"It's altogether right you are, sir," affirmed Freckles heartily. Presently he added, "There's no question but the series is over now."

"Don't think it!" answered McLean. "The Bird Woman is working for success, and success along any line is not won by being scared out. She will be back on the usual day, and ten to one, the Angel will be with her. They are made of pretty stern stuff, and they don't scare worth a cent. Before I left, I told the Bird Woman it would be safe; and it will. You may do your usual walking, but those four guards are there to remain. They are under your orders absolutely. They are prohibited from firing on any bird or molesting anything that you want to protect, but there they remain, and this time it is useless for you to say one word. I have listened to your pride too long. You are too precious to me, and that voice of yours is too precious to the world to run any more risks."

"I am sorry to have anything spoil the series," said Freckles, "and I'd love them to be coming, the Angel especial, but it can't be. You'll have to tell them so. You see, Jack would have been ready to stake his life she meant what she said and did to him. When the teams pulled out, Wessner seized me; then he and Jack went to quarrelling over whether they should finish me then or take me to the next tree they were for felling. Between them they were pulling me around and hurting me bad. Wessner wanted to get at me right then, and Jack said he shouldn't be touching me till the last tree was out and all the rest of them gone. I'm belaving Jack really hated to see me done for in the beginning; and I think, too, he was afraid if Wessner finished me then he'd lose his nerve and cut, and they couldn't be managing the felling without him; anyway, they were hauling me round like I was already past all feeling, and they tied me up again. To keep me courage up, I twits Wessner about having to tie me and needing another man to help handle me. I told him what I'd do to him if I was free, and he grabs up me own club and lays open me head with it. When the blood came streaming, it set Jack raving, and he cursed and damned Wessner for a coward and a softy. Then Wessner turned on Jack and gives it to him for letting the Angel make a fool of him. Tells him she was just playing with him, and beyond all manner of doubt she'd gone after you, and there was nothing to do on account of his foolishness but finish me, get out, and let the rest of the timber go, for likely you was on the way right then. That drove Jack plum crazy.

"I don't think he was for having a doubt of the Angel before, but then he just raved. He grabbed out his gun and turned on Wessner. Spang! It went out of his fist, and the order comes: 'Hands up!' Wessner reached for kingdom come like he was expecting to grab hold and pull himself up. Jack puts up what he has left. Then he leans over to me and tells me what he'll do to me if he ever gets out of there alive. Then, just like a snake hissing, he spits out what he'll do to her for playing him. He did get away, and with his strength, that wound in his hand won't be bothering him long. He'll do to me just what he said, and when he hears it really was she that went after you, why, he'll keep his oath about her.

"He's lived in the swamp all his life, sir, and everybody says it's always been the home of cutthroats, outlaws, and runaways. He knows its most secret places as none of the others. He's alive. He's in there now, sir. Some way he'll keep alive. If you'd seen his face, all scarlet with passion, twisted with pain, and black with hate, and hear him swearing that oath, you'd know it was a sure thing. I ain't done with him yet, and I've brought this awful thing on her."

"And I haven't begun with him yet," said McLean, setting his teeth. "I've been away too slow and too easy, believing there'd be no greater harm than the loss of a tree. I've sent for a couple of first-class detectives. We will put them on his track, and rout him out and rid the country of him. I don't propose for him to stop either our work or our pleasure. As for his being in the swamp now, I don't believe it. He'd find a way out last night, in spite of us. Don't you worry! I am at the helm now, and I'll see to that gentleman in my own way."

"I wish to my soul you had seen and heard him!" said Freckles, unconvinced.

They entered the swamp, taking the route followed by the Bird Woman and the Angel. They really did find the logs, almost where the Angel had predicted they would be. McLean went to the South camp and had an interview with Crowen that completely convinced him that the Angel was correct there also. But he had no proof, so all he could do was to discharge the man, although his guilt was so apparent that he offered to withdraw the wager.

Then McLean sent for a pack of bloodhounds and put them on to the trail of Black Jack. They clung to it, on and on, into the depths of the swamp, leading their followers through what had been considered impassable and impenetrable ways, and finally, around near the west entrance and into the swale. Here the dogs bellowed, raved, and fell over each other in their excitement. They raced back and forth from swamp to swale, but follow the scent farther they would not, even though cruelly driven. At last their owner attributed their actions to snakes, and as they were very valuable dogs, abandoned the effort to urge them on. So that all they really established was the fact that Black Jack had eluded their vigilance and crossed the trail some time in the night. He had escaped to the swale; from there he probably crossed the corduroy, and reaching the lower end of the swamp, had found friends. It was a great relief to feel that he was not in the swamp, and it raised the spirits of every man on the line, though many of them expressed regrets that he who was undoubtedly most to blame should escape, while Wessner, who in the beginning was only his tool, should be left to punishment.

But for Freckles, with Jack's fearful oath ringing in his ears, there was neither rest nor peace. He was almost ill when the day for the next study of the series arrived and he saw the Bird Woman and the Angel coming down the corduroy. The guards of the east line he left at their customary places, but those of the west he brought over and placed, one near Little Chicken's tree, and the other at the carriage. He was firm about the Angel's remaining in the carriage, that he did not offer to have unhitched. He went with the Bird Woman to secure the picture, which was the easiest matter it had been at any time yet, for the simple reason that the placing of the guards and the unusual movement around the swamp had made Mr. and Mrs. Chicken timid, and they had not carried Little Chicken the customary amount of food. Freckles, in the anxiety of the past few days, had neglected him, and he had been so hungry, much of the time, that when the Bird Woman held up a sweet-bread, although he had started toward the recesses of the log at her coming, he stopped; with slightly opened beak, he waited anxiously for the treat, and gave a study of great value, showing every point of his head, also his wing and tail development.

When the Bird Woman proposed to look for other subjects close the line, Freckles went so far as to tell her that Jack had made fearful threats against the Angel. He implored her to take the Angel home and keep her under unceasing guard until Jack was located. He wanted to tell her all about it, but he knew how dear the Angel was to her, and he dreaded to burden her with his fears when they might prove groundless. He allowed her to go, but afterward blamed himself severely for having done so.